He Was Caught In His Own Trap. He Had Wanted To Make Her Love Him, And Instead...

A woman like Noor, vital, beautiful, with a heart now revealed as good and true—how had he left his own heart out of his calculations? What arrogance had blinded him to his vulnerability?

Bari loved her. Fire seemed to burn where his heart had once been.

How could he have imagined himself immune to her?

He shook his head. He had had to learn that he, too, had a heart. And that his heart was a better judge of truth than his intellect.

Could she love him now, when he had imposed such unnecessary suffering on her? When he had ranted at her, blamed her and told her the great lie—that he did not love her?

Such blind foolishness was over now. If only it were not too late....

Dear Reader,

As expected, Silhouette Desire has loads of passionate, powerful and provocative love stories for you this month. Our DYNASTIES: THE DANFORTHS continuity is winding to a close with the penultimate title, *Terms of Surrender,* by Shirley Rogers. A long-lost Danforth heir may just have been found—and heavens, is this prominent family in for a big surprise! And talk about steamy secrets, Peggy Moreland is back with *Sins of a Tanner,* a stellar finale to her series THE TANNERS OF TEXAS.

If it's scandalous behavior you're looking for, look no farther than *For Services Rendered* by Anne Marie Winston. This MANTALK book—the series that offers stories strictly from the hero's point of view—has a fabulous hero who does the heroine a very special favor. Hmmmm. And Alexandra Sellers is back in Desire with a fresh installment of her SONS OF THE DESERT series. *Sheikh's Castaway* will give you plenty of sweet (and naughty) dreams.

Even more shocking situations pop up in Linda Conrad's sensual *Between Strangers.* Imagine if you were stuck on the side of the road during a blizzard and a sexy cowboy offered *you* shelter from the storm…. (Hello, are you still with me?) Rounding out the month is Margaret Allison's *Principles and Pleasures,* a daring romp between a workaholic heroine and a man she doesn't know is actually her archenemy.

So settle in for some sensual, scandalous love stories…and enjoy every moment!

Melissa Jeglinski

Melissa Jeglinski
Senior Editor, Silhouette Desire

Please address questions and book requests to:
Silhouette Reader Service
U.S.: 3010 Walden Ave., P.O. Box 1325, Buffalo, NY 14269
Canadian: P.O. Box 609, Fort Erie, Ont. L2A 5X3

SHEIKH'S CASTAWAY

ALEXANDRA SELLERS

Silhouette® Desire

Published by Silhouette Books

America's Publisher of Contemporary Romance

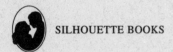 SILHOUETTE BOOKS

ISBN 0-373-76618-1

SHEIKH'S CASTAWAY

Copyright © 2004 by Alexandra Sellers

All rights reserved. Except for use in any review, the reproduction
or utilization of this work in whole or in part in any form by any
electronic, mechanical or other means, now known or hereafter
invented, including xerography, photocopying and recording, or in
any information storage or retrieval system, is forbidden without
the written permission of the editorial office, Silhouette Books,
233 Broadway, New York, NY 10279 U.S.A.

All characters in this book have no existence outside the imagination of
the author and have no relation whatsoever to anyone bearing the same
name or names. They are not even distantly inspired by any individual
known or unknown to the author, and all incidents are pure invention.

This edition published by arrangement with Harlequin Books S.A.

® and TM are trademarks of Harlequin Books S.A., used under license.
Trademarks indicated with ® are registered in the United States Patent
and Trademark Office, the Canadian Trade Marks Office and in other
countries.

Visit Silhouette Books at www.eHarlequin.com

Printed in U.S.A.

Books by Alexandra Sellers

Silhouette Desire

*Sheikh's Ransom #1210
*The Solitary Sheikh #1217
*Beloved Sheikh #1221
Occupation: Casanova #1264
*Sheikh's Temptation #1274
*Sheikh's Honor #1294
*Sheikh's Woman #1341
*The Sultan's Heir #1379
*Undercover Sultan #1385
*Sleeping with the Sultan #1391
*The Playboy Sheikh #1417
*Sheikh's Castaway #1618

*Sons of the Desert

Silhouette Yours Truly

A Nice Girl Like You
Not Without a Wife!
Shotgun Wedding
Occupation: Millionaire

Silhouette Intimate Moments

The Real Man #73
The Male Chauvinist #110
The Old Flame #154
The Best of Friends #348
The Man Next Door #406
A Gentleman and a Scholar #539
The Vagabond #579
Dearest Enemy #635
Roughneck #689
Bride of the Sheikh #771
Wife on Demand #833
Born Royal #1118

ALEXANDRA SELLERS

is the author of over twenty-five novels and a feline language text published in 1997 and still selling.

Born and raised in Canada, Alexandra first came to London, England, as a drama student. Now she lives near Hampstead Heath with her husband, Nick. They share housekeeping with Monsieur, who jumped through the window one day and announced, as cats do, that he was moving in.

I would like to thank the following
for their generously given expert advice and help

Pete Godwin, aviator
Mark Hofton, designer
Jennifer Nauss, friend and editor
Geoff Tetley, life raft specialist
Jo and Dennis Wallace, world sailors

and AVON LIFE RAFTS

I couldn't have done it without you

One

Princess Noor pushed the fold of her bridal veil away from her face with an impatient hand and blinked out the cockpit window, her mouth opening on a soundless breath.

Cloud. A thick, grey-white mass blanketing the distant mainland as far as she could see.

But she had no instrument rating. She couldn't fly in cloud.

"It *can't* be!" she whispered, aghast. Sunlight still glinted merrily from the rich turquoise of the Gulf of Barakat beneath her, but that offered no solution when she had had zero practice putting the little amphibian plane down on water.

Why hadn't she noticed the cloud building up? She should have taken evasive action long ago. Had the yards of billowing tulle on her head confused her vision? Or had the humiliation gnawing at her stomach distracted her?

As if waking out of a dream now, Noor shook her head and looked around.

What was she doing here?

She hadn't even stopped to remove her veil before taking off into the unknown. Hadn't checked the weather. Didn't have a destination. Her only thought had been to put as much distance as she could between herself and marriage to Sheikh Bari al Khalid.

She gazed out at the cloud again, her heart beating fast. She might have put a very permanent distance between them. If that cloud caught up with her, she wouldn't be marrying anyone. Ever.

It had begun—when had it begun? When her parents' families fled their beautiful country in the aftermath of Ghasib's coup thirty-odd years before and both chose Australia? When the two young expatriate Bagestanis who became her parents had fallen in love and married?

Or had it begun only months ago, when the royal family's long struggle to regain the throne had at last been successful, culminating in Sultan Ashraf's now-legendary ride to the gates of the Old Palace through streets crammed with cheering, delirious multitudes?

"We loff heem!" the populace had cried, dancing, singing, laughing and crying, and even a jaded television reporter had unashamedly wiped a tear from her cheek.

Yes, perhaps that was the real beginning. For that was when Noor Ashkani's comfortable, predictable life had been tumbled into a disorder so shocking and startling she seemed to herself to have become a different person.

That was when her father had made his world-shattering announcement. When the family, like so many other exiled Bagestanis around the world, were watching events unfold on television, weeping and hugging each other in a powerful combination of hope, fear and joy, her father had pointed at the image of the stern, noble face of Sultan Ashraf al Jawadi on the screen, and said, "Now it can be told. You are not what you think. He is your cousin."

Cousin! That man on the white horse soon to be crowned Sultan of Bagestan! And not a distant cousin, either. Noor's mother was the daughter of the deposed Sultan Hafzuddin and his second wife, the French-woman named Sonia. Her father was descended from the old Sultan's sister. They owned palaces and property, seized by Ghasib, which would now be returned to them. They were titled.

So no longer was she Noor Ashkani, daughter of a wealthy Bagestani exile who had made good in his adopted country. She was Sheikha Noor Yasmin al Jawadi Durrani, granddaughter of the deposed Sultan of Bagestan, cousin to the present Sultan-to-be, and related to the royal family of the neighbouring kingdom of Parvan, too.

And to prove it, not long after, the new Sultan's invitation to attend the coronation in Bagestan arrived, printed on heavy white paper, with the royal seal that hadn't been seen on official documents for over thirty years.

"More of a command than an invitation," her father had said in satisfaction.

Noor had never in her life seen a sight so moving as that of the royal couple, tall and severely beautiful, glittering with gold, pearls and diamonds, as they slowly paced the red carpet through the halls of the ancient palace past the hundreds of breathlessly silent guests to the throne room.

Sheikh Bari al Khalid had been one of the newly appointed Cup Companions who followed behind the Sultan. Later she learned that he was the grandson of her own grandfather's friend, both of whom, in a time long gone, had been Cup Companions to the old Sultan.

But then he was just one of the twelve most gorgeous men she had ever set eyes on.

Noor keyed the radio mike.

"Matar Filkoh, this is India Sierra Quebec two six."

"Indi…not reading…say again." The radio crackled and spat, giving more static than speech. She must be nearly out of range.

"This is India Sierra Quebec two six," she carefully recited. "Request your current weather, repeat weather."

"Runway in…two, surface wind one eight zero deg…teen gusting thirty-five knots. Bro…at five hundred, heavy…with nimbo…rain…"

The signal broke up completely. Her heart beating hard, Noor signed off and sat for a moment taking stock. If the airport had been clear, there might have been a case for running the risk of trying to get to it through the cloud. But the airport was in the mountains. And with cloud, rain and wind gusting to thirty-five when she got there—if she got there—!

The sky had been clear when she took off. The cloud must have been building in the mountains. Or maybe it had just suddenly formed while she wasn't looking. Cloud could do that, given the right conditions.

Nimbostratus, she was pretty sure he'd said. The really treacherous clouds were cumulonimbus, which carried turbulence, but any cloud was deadly when she had no instrument rating. She didn't even have minimal experience of flying on instruments. There hadn't seemed much point when she flew only recreationally.

Cloud was terrifying because in cloud a pilot could so easily become disorientated. She could simply spiral down out of the sky.

The best alternative was an immediate landing on water. But she had never landed on water.

She had watched an expert do it. That counted for something, Noor reminded herself.

Bari. Involuntarily she glanced down at the pearl-encrusted white silk and lace that covered her breasts. Oh, yes, Bari al Khalid was an expert pilot. An expert at many things, including seduction.

Also an expert liar. But thank God she had found that out in time. Her eyes searched the instrument panel and found the clock. An hour! Was that all it was? If she hadn't heard what she'd heard, hadn't run, Sheikh Bari al Khalid would now be her husband.

At the grand reception after the coronation, powerfully masculine and fierce in a maroon silk jacket, with a glittering jewelled sword at his hip and a thick rope of pearls draped across his chest, of course Bari al Khalid made his presence felt. You couldn't be in the vicinity of so much arrogant masculinity and not notice.

But what drew Noor's attention was the way he kept staring at her, an expression on his face that seemed half passion, half rage. And as if they were attached by an invisible thread that he could not break, he seemed to circle her, so that whenever she looked up, he was always there, at a distance.

Noor was a pretty young woman whose soft, rounded face only hinted at the beauty that would be hers in a few more years, but that day she was stunning. Her parents had called the sky the limit, and Princess Noor was wearing a fabulously expensive *Arabian Nights* dress in pastel green silk from Princess Zara's own favourite designer.

A semitransparent bodice with a high halter neck, glittering with pearls and emeralds, clung to her full breasts and neat waist. Beneath, a cloud of multitoned layers of green silk swathed her legs, half skirt, half harem pants. And in a seductive mockery of the traditional veil, transparent tulle cascaded from the back of her head to her feet, caught in as if haphazardly at her waist to cloak her bare arms.

Noor's makeup was flawless, her dark auburn hair burnished, waving back from her temples and forehead to show small, perfect ears and emphasize the softly rounded chin and smooth, slender neck.

And all around, people were calling her "Your Highness."

But still, she was a little overwhelmed to think that an oak of a man like Bari al Khalid had taken one look and come crashing to earth.

The shadow of the little plane danced over the bright waves below as Noor grappled with her dilemma. She had put this plane down on land, albeit with Bari in the copilot's seat. She knew how it handled. If she had to, she would give a liquid landing her best shot.

But if there was another way… She pulled out the chart and tried to estimate her position. With the cloud obliterating all landmarks except the tips of the mountains, it wasn't easy.

Should she try an immediate landing? It would mean a lot of empty sea for someone to search when she needed rescue afterwards. Should she risk flying closer to land—closer to the cloud bank—before landing? What if the cloud suddenly swept out and grabbed her while she was putting down?

There was another problem: Noor was used to landing only where she had good visual conditions. She would become disoriented with nothing but the altimeter to tell her how close the surface was.

The sea was so deceptive. She might hit the water when she thought she was a hundred feet up. Or the reverse—what she thought was a ripple on the surface might be a ten-foot swell.

Like Bari al Khalid, she thought. *I thought I was close to him, but all the time he was miles away.*

The Cup Companion was introduced to his lord's cousin as a matter of protocol. He bowed formally, one hand a fist at his breast, but his expression was anything but formal. The arrogant sexual confidence in his black eyes melted her where she stood.

"Come," Sheikh al Khalid had ordered, in fine autocratic command, as if she could have no wishes different from his own. "I will show you the gardens. You will admire the fountains."

Noor had never been swept off her feet before. And she knew it could never happen again with such thrilling panache, such heady excitement. During the weeks she stayed in Bagestan, discovering the homeland of her parents, Bari monopolized her time, and never before in her largely fun-filled life had she had so much fun.

Bari was expert at everything. He played demon tennis, his dark body so lithe and muscled she was watching him when she should have kept her eyes on the ball, took her sailing on the most beautiful and perfectly seaworthy little yacht she'd ever seen, allowed her to pilot his private plane, escorted her to fabulous parties with the rich and famous that until now had been out of her reach, kept her constantly laughing….

And made intoxicating love to her for the first time in that small sailing yacht at the height of a storm. Noor had been a virgin, but that moment had answered all her dreams. Oh, it had been worth waiting for!

"Of course you will marry me," he told Noor, his voice harsh with passion. "We will make our life and raise our children in Bagestan."

It was far too soon; of course it was. Her cousin Jalia said it, and Jalia was right. But Noor's head was whirling. Everything on her personal horizon seemed to have changed in one heartbeat. In the sea of confusion that had surrounded her since her father's announcement, she had one spar—that Bari wanted her. That Bari was sure, and knew what he was doing.

She had flown home only to make her arrangements and return to Bagestan for the huge wedding, organized with breathtaking speed, that practically all of Barakati and Bagestani society would be attending.

And then, with the ceremony only minutes away, her one spar had been torn from her. She had learned what a fool she was, what a fool he was making of her.

Bari knew what he was doing, all right, but he didn't love her. He wasn't marrying her for love. He didn't even want to marry her.

The islands! her brain suddenly shouted at her. *There are islands out here!* How could she have forgotten that? She had flown over the scattered group of islands with Bari. *Al Jeza'ir al Khaleej,* he had called them. The Gulf Islands.

"They have been uninhabited since the forced evacuation," he had told her. "Except the biggest, which has a luxury hotel complex. The Gulf Eden was one of the ways Ghasib drew foreign currency into his coffers. Built by a huge international hotel chain to cater to very wealthy foreigners."

His tone had been filled with contempt, and Noor had dropped her eyes and omitted to mention that she had almost gone there herself once. Only her father's absolute diktat had stopped her.

This looks like my chance at last, she told herself dryly. But where were the islands? How far away? Her eyes dropped to the chart again, searching. *Please, God, show me a way out of this.*

Two

Sheikh Bari al Khalid lifted his head and watched his runaway bride over the back of the passenger seat separating the cockpit from the luggage space where he was hidden.

How dared she abandon their wedding in such a way? How dared she run away from him like this? Without a word—no announcement, no explanation, not even so much as a blink of apology!

What sort of man did she think he was, to put up with such insult?

The heady mix of fury, shock and disbelief—if that were all!—that had driven his actions was now, however, tinged with grim amusement. So the airport was clouded over. That was a dangerous situation: his bashful bride couldn't fly in cloud, and she couldn't land on water.

How richly she deserved this dilemma!

She was a fool to have chosen this method of escape.

The weather had been volatile and unpredictable ever since the ending of the drought a few weeks ago, a fact she knew well. As an inexperienced pilot she should never have risked coming up alone.

A sardonic smile stretched his mouth, making him aware of how his jaw was clenched. He would like to leave her longer in this predicament, teach her a sharp lesson. Hell, he'd like to hide here till she was on her last gallon of fuel and begging fate for release. How he would enjoy seeing her desperate with regret and remorse!

But he couldn't risk it. Her calm might give way to panic without warning. And a few seconds of that would be enough to kill them.

No, Noor clearly couldn't be trusted to keep her head in the face of adversity.

Her head? She couldn't even be trusted to keep her word!

Well, she would be made to keep it. Of that he was determined. She would not escape. She had promised herself to him, and she would keep her promise.

He stood up and moved forward between the rear seats. "Caught in your own trap," he snarled when he was behind her. "What did you expect?"

"Bari?!" Noor's gasp sounded like tearing silk against the hum of the engine. Her head snapped up and she blankly took in the glaring black eyes, the darkly handsome face, the imposing figure magnificently sheathed in purple silk and draped with pearls. His dress sword hung from his hip.

She frowned. "Damn! I'm hallucinating!"

"I wish you were!" he said between his teeth. "I wish we were both hallucinating! Insanity would be preferable to learning what kind of woman you are!"

He lifted the bundle of her veil that nestled in the

right-hand seat and tossed it onto the floor behind her with fierce contempt, as if this symbol of their wedding made his stomach heave. Noor felt its drag against the headdress of fresh white roses still pinned to her hair.

Then, expertly manoeuvring the jewel-encrusted scabbard, he edged into the space and sat. With a deliberation that somehow infuriated her, he buckled himself into the harness.

"I have control," he announced formally and, with unhurried grace, his actions completely distanced from his vengeful mood, he engaged the secondary controls. The plane responded to its master's touch with a purr.

"Are you real?" Noor asked, wondering, *Am I totally crazy?* She had resigned control to what might be only a phantom. Was this why planes fell from the sky without explanation? Because the man flying it existed only in someone's desperate imagination?

"You will see how real I am," Bari growled. She had never seen that generous, sensuous mouth so narrowed. He must be real. Why would her mind trouble to conjure up a vision that only terrified her further?

"I guess you're the answer to my prayer!" she realized with a jerky laugh. "Some sense of humour God has!"

"Do you call this scenario God's doing? You are fool enough to think that, in acting like a barbarian, you carry out God's will?"

His tone was scathing, and her flesh shivered as the first delicate tendrils of shame reached through her blind panic to touch Noor's soul.

Bari's eyes moved to the instrument panel. Since she was in the pilot's seat, he had to crane. She felt the plane alter course in a broad arc, out over the sparkling sea. There was no cloud in this direction, but even if it caught up with them, she knew Bari was fully rated on instruments.

"How did you get here? You just materialized?"

His voice whipped her. "Do you imagine it was difficult to trail a white limousine with a bridal veil streaming from the sunroof through the streets? Nor was it difficult to guess that you planned to take the plane."

He was wrong there. She hadn't planned it. She had driven to the plane only when she realized that in her panicked flight she had taken nothing with her, neither her handbag nor a change of clothes. She had to have cash, but she didn't dare go to the palace—it would be the first place they looked for her. And if they found her, they'd take her back to the wedding.

The thought of returning back among the wedding guests, having to explain herself when no explanation would be good enough, had appalled her. Then she had remembered that Bari kept emergency fuel money in a secret compartment in the plane. In the swamp into which she had cast herself, she had grabbed at that one frail straw.

She had discovered the plane fuelled and ready for their honeymoon journey. Only then had the thought of flying away from the impossible problems she'd created suddenly and crazily occurred to her.

"Only the why of such barbarian, uncivilized behaviour escaped me." The words came at her in sharp, broken shards, as if he chewed up glass as he spoke. "Even a child raised in the streets would hesitate to act as you have done!"

His contempt came out through lips that had practically disappeared. Noor flinched. She had never seen such an expression on his face before. She had never seen anyone so angry, and she had to admit he had some cause. But she couldn't accept such wholesale criticism, such overwhelming blame.

"You got to the plane ahead of me, and instead of talking to me you hid, and you're calling *me* childish?" she snapped.

"No doubt you would have relished a public confrontation, Noor, but I did not. We will return to the house and you will marry me without comment, or any public airing of your unforgivable actions."

"Return to the house?" Her voice climbed in startled objection as she suddenly realized he had been altering course to fly back to Bagestan. She straightened with a jerk. "What are you doing? Where are you going?"

"We will land at the dock and walk up to the house and apologize to our guests for the delay. Then we will take our vows," he said with the clarity that only the coldest fury can impart. "A little late. But the bride is allowed that, I believe."

She stared at him. What arrogance! Noor's doubts about her behaviour were conveniently swamped in outrage. "Maybe you didn't notice that the bride changed her mind, Bari! I'm not going to marry you!"

"You did not change your mind," he informed her contemptuously. "You would not be acting like this if you had ever intended to marry me, of course. But you chose the wrong man. I do not play these Western games, Noor. You said you would marry me. You will do so."

"It's no game! Turn this plane around!" she screeched. How dare he brush her off when he must know her reasons for what she did? At the very least, he suspected! Who did he think he was?

"Who do you think—"

"It will not take long. You may pass the time by telling me what it is, if not a game. And I will have the truth."

"The truth! Oh, that's good, that is! *I'm* not the one who's been lying from beginning to end of this whole affair! I'm not the one with zero conscience! Suppose *you* begin by telling—"

"Do *you* talk to *me* about conscience?" he shouted, as if suddenly losing his grip on a fierce control. Her heart gave a nervous kick; his temper was at white heat. "What has been your motive in pretending to agree to marry me and then playing such a terrible trick? Hundreds of people have come—"

"You must have a very good guess as to what motivated me! Your lies! You must have known I'd find out the truth soon—"

"—from all over the world to celebrate not just our wedding but their hopes for the rebirth of our country!"

"—er or later! I guess you were counting on later! Too bad!"

"Do you know you nearly ran into the Sultan's motorcade as you drove out the gates? He and the Sultana—"

"The Bagestani flags on the fenders gave me a hint," Noor admitted. "He hires good outriders, your boss. They nearly drove me off the road."

He turned on her a gaze so black with threat she cowered. "Do not speak slightingly to me of a man of whose courage and strength you are ignorant."

The plane had turned 130 degrees, and the expanse of cloud covering the mainland suddenly came into view again out the window behind her head.

Bari's eyes widened, and then narrowed. How had he let his anger suck him into argument when he should have been watching the sky?

Noor turned to follow the direction of his gaze and let out a breath of stunned surprise. Bari had made his appearance not a minute too soon. The cloud had built fast and was rushing towards them.

If I were alone now, I'd be saying my last prayers.

"Cumulonimbus," the dark-eyed Sheikh murmured softly. "I am a thousand fools."

She gasped hoarsely, her hand lifting to press against the window in protest as she stared out at the sinister mass that approached.

But Bari was right.

"The airport said nimbostratus!" she cried.

He made no reply, except to the threat they faced. He was throttling back.

Cumulonimbus clouds were dangerous even to the most experienced instrument-trained pilot. They could carry severe turbulence. Turbulence might easily cause the plane to break up.

The plane began to lose height, and she felt it alter course again, away from the coastline. Of course he would try to get under the cloud, Noor realized. If only he could…

"Not even the sense to remove your lace finery before taking off into cloud!" he said harshly, his eyes on the instrument panel. The acres of silk and tulle surrounding his ex-bride didn't make his task any easier. "In the water, it would drag you down to certain death. Get rid of it."

His air of cold command was completely new. Noor gnawed her lip at that *in the water,* for it seemed to make the danger real. While he tried fruitlessly to raise air traffic control, she lifted her hands and frantically began to pull out the first of dozens of pins fixing the wreath of white roses in her hair, though if the plane broke up in the air it wouldn't be her bride's finery that killed her.

Abruptly, sea and sky and sun disappeared, and the little plane entered a world all grey. Noor heard a strange, quiet shushing. Droplets of water appeared on the glass.

Her fingers trembled and hesitated, then went on with their task. What else was there to do? Bari was in command of the situation as far as that was possible, and to offer resistance—or even help—now would be ridiculous.

Bari leaned over to peer at an instrument, and she distantly noted how a dark curl gleamed in the reflected glow from the panel. What a powerfully handsome man he was! Noor thought involuntarily. Not conventional, Hollywood handsome—he wasn't even at handshaking distance with the bland, polished looks that passed for masculinity on a movie screen. No, Bari was one of Saladin's warriors. Fierce nobility was what shaped his jaw, not pineapple facials and a perfectly judged beard shadow. If only...

But now was not the moment for such thoughts.

At last the flowers and tulle began to come loose, and Noor ignored the remaining pins and dragged at the headdress, wincing at the pain as hair came away with it. She tossed it over her shoulder onto the floor behind, where it sank into the nest of itself.

A faint, delicate perfume floated to her nostrils from the bruised roses. Her senses, it seemed, were heightened. Her fingers unconsciously massaging her protesting scalp, Noor picked out the pins that were still caught, combing through her hair, trying not to remember the excited, happy moment when the hairdresser had set the wreath on her head.

Without warning, a fierce gust of wind smacked them. The plane rocked, and so did her heart.

"*Ya Allah!*" Bari exclaimed, and the grey all around them abruptly turned dark. Another sharp slap of wind.

Then, much more ominously, a low rumble.

Horror shivered down her spine. Noor's heart lurched in frantic denial and her mouth was suddenly dry as the desert. It wasn't possible! *Please, God, let it not...*

Another crack of thunder cut her off. A thunderstorm. And they were in it.

Three

There are few things more dangerous than a thunderstorm embedded in cloud, and Noor knew it. It is the pilot's nightmare.

She might have chosen death not only for herself, but for Bari. Her heart thudded with useless regret.

"Are you strapped in tight?"

His voice was so calm it shocked her, an incongruity her mind couldn't cope with. It had the effect of setting her building panic at bay.

"No. My dress—"

"Damn your dress." She could feel that the plane was still descending, but there seemed no bottom to the cloud. "Get your harness on. Fast."

Though a stubborn part of her resented his autocratic tone, she knew it would be insane to resist. Noor twisted in her seat, groping underneath the swathes of silk for the webbing of her harness.

The plane was still losing altitude.

"Are we landing?"

"We'll see," Bari said dryly as another crack of noise drowned him out. She thought she sensed him adjust his heading again, but how he had any idea where they were, she couldn't imagine.

She had never seen Bari operating under pressure before. It surprised her that such a passionate, hot-tempered man could be so cool under fire. For a brief moment the thought of her only experience of his—of any man's—passion flicked across her mind. He hadn't been cool then...or had he? That must have been faked, too.

Her fingers quickly found one buckle, but the other eluded her. Noor half stood in the confined space and groped the seat behind her.

Bari reached across and fielded the buckle of her harness, holding it for her in one strong, well-formed hand. *Well, at least I won't die a virgin!* The thought rose unbidden, and a breath of laughter—and something else—escaped her. Her eyes brushed up to his as she took the harness from him with a murmur of thanks, but the look she met was hard and ungiving, and the only passion was rejection.

"Even in the lion's mouth," he mocked her.

A jolt of turbulence wiped any retort from her mind. She tumbled back into her seat to the sound of tearing. Her arm hit painfully on something, but Noor suppressed the automatic grunt that rose in her throat and buckled herself in. The webbing abraded the delicate white silk across her breast, tearing the clustered pearl embroidery.

She was sorry about that—it was a beautiful creation.

A pearl fell like a teardrop. A second followed, landing in her palm. Noor's fingers involuntarily caught it, massaged the cool little sphere between finger and thumb. How completely her dreams were being destroyed. And yet…

If they had gone through with the wedding, there would have come a point when they sat side by side in the plane like this. The thought gave her a curious sensation of being in two lives at once. Was there a parallel universe in which they had been married? That other life seemed so close. She could almost feel it, as if she might blink and find everything the same, but different.

Would she have gone on believing Bari loved her, living her fool's dream? Would he have kept up the pretence once he had what he wanted, or would she have learned immediately that he had made a fool of her? Would she ever have guessed if she hadn't overheard the truth…

"She's so spoiled! All she cares about is clothes and jewellery and having a good time. She's just totally frivolous!"

Noor had been standing at the mirror, layers of silk and lace surrounding her, her tanned skin and auburn hair gleaming like the rich heart of a white rose, when the bitchy malice filtered through from the room beyond.

"And I don't believe she's in love with anyone but herself!"

And just like a droplet of dew on the rose's heart was the fabulous al Khalid diamond. Bari's grandfather's wedding gift to her had simply taken her breath away. Noor was used to wealth and all its pleasures, but Bari's family fortune went beyond wealth. The diamond was the biggest single stone Noor had ever seen, and it lay against her hand with a dark fire that almost burned her— like Bari's eyes, she thought with a delicious flutter.

"She is young yet."

"She's twenty-four. Why are you making excuses for her?"

Noor let it wash over her. She had heard it before, directly or implied. The women in Bari's family were not uniformly delighted with his choice of bride, but what should she care about that?

"She has been raised by overfond parents, it's true," said the more placid voice of Bari's aunt. "But she is an al Jawadi by blood. She has more depth than she knows yet."

Of course they didn't know she could hear. She was in the large, luxurious bathroom set between her bedroom and another. A moment ago Noor had been at the centre of buzzing activity, the hair stylist and the makeup artist competing with the dressmaker and her personal maid for her attention, but now, with the excuse of one last nervous visit to the toilet, she had stepped in here to be alone for a moment and catch her breath.

And she had heard voices murmuring together in bitchy comfort in the other bedroom.

"He's only known her a few weeks," the younger one was still protesting, and Noor wondered if this particular cousin, whoever it was, was in love with Bari herself.

"You are talking like a true Westerner. Why should a man know his bride? It is enough that his family knows her family."

In a moment she would go back into her bedroom to face the renewed onslaught of perfectionism from her dressers and wait for Jalia and her bridesmaids to tap on the door to tell her it was time. Time to be escorted to meet the richest, the handsomest, the sexiest man ever to have deserved the title "Cup Companion," the man who had known he wanted to marry Noor Ashkani—Princess Noor Yasmin al Jawadi Durrani—practically from the first glance.

"It's different when the marriage is arranged, though, isn't it?" The murmurs in the next room grew louder as the two women moved past the slightly open door, in complete ignorance of the fact that the subject under discussion was on the other side of it. "Then the families at least have—"

"How is it different? This marriage might not have been arranged in the traditional way, but it was your grandfather who chose the bride."

"Really?" The younger voice sounded both shocked and deliciously intrigued, and Noor's eyes widened with startled dismay. "You mean Bari isn't in love with her?"

She sounded thrilled, Noor noted. Cow.

"He was very bitter when his grandfather told him what was necessary." The voices faded again and she heard the opening of the door that led onto the broad, shady balcony.

"How—but why would Bari agree to something like that? He's so independent!"

"Bari has no choice." The other voice was matter-of-fact. "If he wants the right to the property in Bagestan and the money to restore it, he has to marry as he is instructed. Your grandfather wants an alliance with the Durranis. He will leave the property away from Bari if—"

The door shut, cutting the voices off, and leaving Noor stunned and as white as her veil among the broken pieces of her stupid, childish dreams....

A loud rumble brought her back into the here and now, with all its dangers. Oh, if only her father had never told them their history! If only she could return to her ordinary life, and never learn whose blood ran in her veins. *Princess!* They had been happy as they were! And now...her life had so changed that it might end here, miles from her home, in the next few minutes.

Another, louder crack of thunder, and she bit back a cry. She had seen flickering light within the roiling darkness. If lightning struck…

They hit turbulence and dropped for a few metres before landing with a sickening thud on a boiling air mass. Her stomach churned. *Oh, let me not throw up!* she begged feverishly.

Lightning danced perilously in the black cloud again, and the noise was deafening. They were at the heart of the storm.

Bari struggled against turbulence, hoping he had a heading towards the Gulf Islands as he came down, but he was far from certain. The instruments were jumping so much they were all but useless. And as a mere human he was in the maelstrom, archetypal Chaos, the place where the ordinary senses were powerless as guides.

Flying by the seat of your pants, they called it. *On a wing and a prayer.* The clichés recited themselves in his head, describing truths no one with sense wanted to discover for himself.

He had been acting like a fool for too long. His judgement had been faulty ever since hearing his grandfather's ultimatum, and what a pity he could only recognize that now!

But this wasn't the moment to fan the flames of his legitimate anger, either with his grandfather or with Noor. His mind needed to be clear of everything except the job at hand.

He could keep dropping lower to try to get below the cloud, but that was risky: some of the islands were high and rugged. And even at the coast the foothills were over a thousand feet high in places. So whether he was badly off course or right where he hoped he was, there was terrible risk involved in flying low.

But to continue to fly inside the storm invited even more certain disaster. He had to take the risk and try to put down, trusting that he would break out of cloud in time to see where he was and take evasive action if it wasn't where he hoped.

Noor's mouth was dry. Her heart beat with terror; the metallic taste of panic was on her tongue. She had never been afraid for her life before. They could be struck by lightning. Turbulence could break the plane apart. They could fall from the sky like a stone.

Or the earth could leap up in their path and smash them to atoms.

She wanted to lash out and hit something; her legs were tense with the need to run screaming from the scene. She wanted her heart to stop thundering in her chest and cheeks and temples. She wanted to wake up from this nightmare and find herself safe.

"Oh God!" she whimpered as a fist of sound punched the little plane and set it juddering. How was it possible one tiny act had set such a chain of events in motion? If she could have it to do over again…

"Pray for some common sense while you're at it," Bari advised with grim humour. He was fighting to hold the plane against the turbulence, and he seemed to have as good a grip on himself as on the controls.

The injustice of the comment infuriated her—or was it the justice of it?—and as if that fury somehow served as an antidote to the emotion that engulfed her, Noor gritted her teeth in sudden revulsion for her own fear. If this was death, she wasn't meeting it as a coward! She wasn't going to spend her last few minutes in a panic, pleading with fate or regretting her own stupidity or anything else.

The noise was deafening now—the shriek of wind,

the rain and thunder and the protesting engine all con-
spiring together to produce cacophony. Noor ran her
eyes over the instrument panel. Even if they hadn't
been leaping around like drops of water on a summer
pavement, the instruments would have told her exactly
nothing.

"There must be something I can do!" she cried over
the noise.

Bari's eyes were steady on her for a moment, clock-
ing the shift in her state of mind. He indicated the radio
with his chin.

"Try and raise air traffic control again," he shouted,
less because he thought it likely than to give her something to do. "Give them our stats. Height eleven hundred and descending. Bearing two two five. See if they
have us on radar and can confirm our position."

But the radio responded with static. They were out
of range, but that told them nothing with regard to their
own position—except that a mountain might be between them and the airport. In the distance she heard the
pilot of another plane saying he could hear her, but the
signal faded and he didn't respond to her call.

"Go to the distress channel," Bari ordered, and a
thrill of renewed fear zinged through her. Every pilot
knew the channel number, but not in the expectation of
ever needing it. Her mouth dry, Noor turned the dial to
read 121.5. She coughed.

"Mayday, May—" she began hoarsely.

Suddenly there was a flash of light all around them,
as though they had touched an electric grid. Then a curious silence, as if the rain were taking a breath, or her
heart had stopped beating. Then rippling, cracking,
booming thunder.

"Did that hit us?" Noor barely breathed the question.

Bari shrugged. "The electrics are still working." He pulled back on the throttle, slowing the engine further.

"I'm going to put down. The sea will be choppy, but better to break up on the surface than up here."

If the sea was beneath them.

Noor felt a sudden calm. *Mash'allah.* "All right. What should I do?"

"There's a life raft in the rear." He sounded doubtful. "Can you get it out?"

She set down the mike and unbuckled herself. "Right."

"Be prepared for more turbulence."

She hastily kicked off her shoes and got up, scrabbling her way between the two passenger seats behind and into the back of the aircraft as fast as she could, yanking at the voluminous skirt of her dress, clutching tightly to anything within reach. Meanwhile the plane leaped and bounced as the storm did its unholy best to knock her off balance.

Strange, she thought distantly, all this bucking wasn't making her queasy now. Maybe having nerves at a fever pitch had something to do with that.

Still the wind howled and shrieked around the little plane. Lightning crackled within the clouds, and the answering thunder pounded and banged them almost physically.

In the luggage space behind the passenger seats, she saw a suitcase-sized container fitted to the bulkhead on a mounting. There were very similar items on the yachts of friends, and in her carefree life Noor had been miles from imagining she would ever actually need one.

She knelt into the cloud of her dress and wrestled with the clasps holding the case in the cradle. She noted only distantly that the tip of one perfect peach-coloured fingernail snapped off in the process.

"LIFE RAFT, 4 PERSON. DO NOT INFLATE IN AN EN-CLOSED SPACE."

Bari swore as the plane bucked again, and Noor fell against the seat and then the bulkhead as she dragged the case awkwardly off its mounting. It was heavy and hard and had a mind of its own, but with curses and tears she at last manoeuvred it to a position behind Bari's seat. Two more fingernails tore in the process.

The sweat of struggle was on Bari's forehead, and his face was white with strain. A black curl fell over one eye. "Sit down," he called. "We'll break out of cloud soon and I may have to take it back up fast."

Fear rushed through her again at this stark statement of what she already knew—that they might be blindly flying towards a mountainside. Biting her lip, Noor struggled back into her seat and shoved her arms through the safety harness, clicking it home.

Rain pounded the metal body of the plane, and the wind screamed around them, in an intensity of sound she'd never heard before. Thunder rolled all around. She felt the noise in her skin, in her body, as if sound itself embraced her, a physical thing.

She picked up the mike again. *"Mayday, Mayday, this is India Sierra—"*

Suddenly they were out of cloud, driving through rain so heavy there was scarcely any improvement in visibility. But below she could see water, and she let her breath out on a long silent sigh. Thank God, thank God. *Alhamdolillah.* She glanced at Bari, but she saw no emotion other than fierce concentration on his face.

"Brace yourself," he said briefly. The water looked choppy and unforgiving. Noor pushed her free hand against the control panel, pressed her stockinged feet against the floor.

"This is India Sierra Quebec two six, we are—"

He slowed the engine, dropping lower, trying to gauge the height of the chop by what he knew of the sea as a sailor. It was rougher than he had hoped.

The belly of the plane touched down with a hollow thump, and then another and another as they hit the waves. Bari wrestled to keep the plane from nose-diving, the muscles of his arms bulging with the effort. As he slowed to a standstill, a bigger swell grabbed the starboard wing. With a sharp, terrifying scream of metal the plane slewed around, bounced up, smacked down, pitched forward and then dropped back.

Four

The high scream stopped. The propellers stopped. The pounding rain increased in ferocity, but still it sounded like silence to the two in the cockpit. Bari slapped his harness open.

"Are you hurt?" His voice was harsh.

"No," Noor said faintly. The truth was she was so shocked that if she did have broken bones she wouldn't have known.

"The hull is damaged," Bari said, flinging open his door onto driving rain and waves that slapped against the belly of the plane, stretching greedy fingers into the cockpit. "We've got a couple of minutes before it goes under."

Noor, dizzy and shaken, struggled out of the harness and her seat again.

Bari was in the open doorway, the rain slashing at him, staining his jacket dark, plastering it to his skin. He tied the cord from the life raft to a metal brace with quick expertise. Somehow he did not look incongruous in his wedding finery. The purple silk jacket that was dress uniform to a Cup Companion only emphasized his physical power and masculinity. Around his hips the jewelled belt of his sword glowed dully. He looked like an ancient painting of a noble warrior, ready for anything.

Lightning crackled behind his head, and thunder exploded around them like a small bomb.

"Take your dress off," he shouted.

Her hand went unconsciously to her throat. "But I'm—"

"Now!" His voice was harsh. "Do you want to drown?"

She was too stunned by events to argue. He was right. If she fell into the water, the dress would drag her down. Anyway, what did she have to hide from Bari? He had been so intimate with her body he practically owned it.

Bari didn't waste time watching to see her obey. He dragged the life raft through the opening and heaved it onto the water.

Noor reached up behind her neck and her fingers tugged at the first of the dozens of tiny silk-covered buttons that ran down her back. She managed to undo three or four, watching as Bari jerked at the cord of the plastic case now riding the waves a short distance away, but the dress was too tight for her to reach further.

"You'll have to undo me," she said hoarsely, and so quietly he didn't hear against the sudden hissing and snapping as the life raft opened. Noor coughed. Since trying to make the Mayday call she seemed to have no voice.

"You have to undo me!" she cried louder.

He looked at her. She was offering her back, her head turned to look over her shoulder into his face. Bari's

eyes took in the lifted shoulder, the fall of glowing auburn hair, the partly opened neckline of the dress, the
soft skin of her back as it disappeared under the delicate white silk.

Even now, with danger crackling all around, the
thought of the might-have-been passed over them.
Wordlessly his hands rose to the buttons, and moved
against her back to undo her wedding dress…as he
might have done in a hushed bedroom somewhere, their
hearts beating not with fear but desire….

He undid two of the tiny, impossible buttons, and
then muttered something she didn't hear. His hands
clenched against her skin for a moment before he
wrenched them apart. The fabric screamed its protest at
the violation of the should-have-been, and he tore the
dress open from neck to hip. Buttons flew like little
pellets, landing all around with a sound that was curiously distinct against the noise of the storm.

They said not a word. Bari lifted his hands and turned
back to his task with the raft. It was nearly fully inflated
now, and he quickly picked up a small satchel as water
began to seep into the plane, staining the carpet with a
warning that time was short.

Noor dragged the dress off, down her arms and over
her hips. Clutching hard on the seat back against the
rocking of the waves, she let it drop with a swoosh to
the floor and stepped out of it. Now she was wearing
nothing but a teddy and stockings.

She dragged the heavy weight of the dress up and flung
it over her arm, and then stood waiting for his signal.

There was a loud pop as the bright red canopy
snapped into place over the raft. Bari held the raft close
to the battered plane, and she watched him toss the
sheathed sword and the satchel through the canopy en-

trance. The eyes that glanced over her were clinically impersonal. Not even by a tightening of his mouth did he seem to remember that the last time he had seen her like this lovemaking had followed.

Lightning crackled between earth and sky, and the black clouds roiled as thunder echoed across the water. A gust of wind smacked them, causing the plane to make a terrifying shift.

"Shoes?" Bari shouted.

"Off."

"Jump onto the canopy."

She clutched her dress and prepared to leap. "What the hell's that for?" he demanded harshly.

"It's all the clothes I have!" she screamed against the turmoil. Without waiting for his approval, she leaped out, and landed spread-eagled on the canopy. It collapsed under her, and she banged her knee painfully on something underneath.

Noor almost panicked then, but when she looked towards Bari he was unmoved by the accident. The life raft rose and fell on the waves for a few seconds while the drenching rain came down, and the heavens roared and flashed.

"Get over!" Bari called. Her dress was everywhere, and she feverishly grabbed at it, rolling it into a bundle with one arm as she clutched desperately to a rope with the other and tried to make room for him.

Her bundled wedding veil landed with a thump, so Bari had seen logic in her decision. A moment later, he landed beside her.

"Get through the entrance—we've got to get the canopy up!" he cried, and for a moment she stared at him in confusion.

Under his rapid-fire direction, dragging her dress

and veil with her, Noor slithered through the entrance hole and under the flattened canopy as if into a sleeping bag, while Bari clung on precariously. Rain poured unmercifully into her face where she lay looking up at the churning black sky. There was something hard and uncomfortable under her thigh.

Bari edged closer, then slid headfirst through the hole beside her. To Noor's amazement, the canopy popped back into place, and suddenly they were inside.

Bari instantly jackknifed up, grabbing at her butt, and choking the sigh of relief in her throat. "What—?" she began.

She saw him heft the sword in the scabbard. He shoved it out the entrance and drew out the sword, tossing the scabbard to fall inside.

The action, the speed of it, choked her.

"Bari!" she screamed hoarsely.

With his free hand he reached for the rope that tethered them to the downed plane, and lifted the sword over it.

A huge swell slapped against the plane without warning, shifting it violently, dragging the rope out of his hand. Bari, the sword held high, was suddenly hanging precariously over the water. A wave lifted the little raft.

"Bari!" Noor shrieked again, in a very different tone. She flung herself on him, grabbed the jewelled sword belt he still wore, and held on tight. The raft slipped dangerously down into the lee of the wave.

He twisted in her hold, his back arching out over the swollen sea, his sword upraised, with rain pouring over him, looking like some ancient painting of a blood-crazed warrior. He stared at her in disbelief as she clung shrieking to his hips. The rain was so drenching she could hardly see, but she got the outrage in his eyes.

"Get back! You'll overturn us!" he ordered furiously.

Noor lifted her hands as if the belt were hot, and slid back inside, wiping the rain and hair from her eyes, her heart beating in tumult as she watched him.

Bari cut the cord that tied them to the plane and moved back inside. He wiped the sword uselessly against his wet sleeve, sheathed it carefully in the confined space and set it down.

Something beside her head on the canopy caught her eye. Her eyes sparkling, she said, "There appears to be a little knife stuck to the canopy here, Bari. I suppose not everyone is expected to be carrying their own ceremonial sword."

She caught the glimmer of a smile, of the old, humorous Bari, but there was no time for laughter. The sea smashed over them, the little raft rose with a sickening swoop, and the moment was lost. With a loud, terrifying complaint from the torn wing, the plane shifted again. Would they be dragged with it?

A red polythene bag was tied to the floor. Bari wrestled the neck open, then drew out a small plastic scoop and fixed a metal handle to it. Everything he did was quick, with an air of urgency that only heightened her anxiety. A breath of nervous laughter escaped her.

"What's that for?"

Bari tossed it down.

"Never used a paddle before?" he asked. "You'd better learn fast."

With a neat economy of motion he pulled another one out of the sack and fitted that together.

"Shouldn't we close the entrance? We're getting a lot of water in here," Noor complained.

"There's work to be done first. Pick that up and come and help me."

All her life Noor had been pampered. The only girl,

and the youngest child, she had always been special. No one made real demands of her. Her needs were always met through someone else's work—servants, her parents, her brothers, even her cousin Jalia had all conspired to cushion her against the truth that life required effort. Any effort Noor made went in the direction of fun.

And no one—including Bari—had ever spoken to her in the tones he was using now.

"What's the point? Where are we trying to get to? We don't even know where we are!"

"We know we're too damned close to the plane, and it's sinking," he informed her flatly. "We have no time to argue. Try to spread your weight as much as possible. It's dangerous to have all the weight on one side, but we have no choice."

Bari pushed his head and shoulders out into the rain and began to paddle, fighting to get the raft away from the downed plane. It lay helpless in the water, with its ugly broken wing, and their position was dangerous— a wave could smash them against the hull. Or they might be caught by the wing, or hammered by the tail, as the plane went under.

Or simply sucked down with it when it went.

After a moment, to his surprise, Noor moved up behind him and put her head out, paddle at the ready.

"What do I do?" she shrieked against the storm.

His biceps bulged under the soaking-wet jacket. "We'll aim to get around the nose and out that way," he shouted.

Noor could hardly see, hardly breathe in the downpour, but he had challenged her and she wasn't going to give in. She wiped her hair out of her eyes and tried again.

"Watch my paddle," Bari ordered, and that made it easier. Looking down she could follow the direction of his paddling, and she got less rain in her eyes.

They paddled together, side by side, wordlessly battling the waves that tried to drag them towards the sinking plane. Then suddenly, pushed close and then swept on by a high swell, they were past it and out of danger.

"That's good enough," Bari said. They drew back inside, and he rolled up the door flap and sealed it, and now at last they were cocooned against the storm. Soaking wet, Noor reflected, and chilled, and in a tiny space that was awash with water and bouncing like forty miles of bad road, but suddenly it seemed like comfort. She slumped down against the rounded side of the raft, panting, her heart drumming in her ears, and realized what a relative thing comfort was.

For a minute or two they rested in silence as their breathing calmed. Then Bari opened the flap again and looked out, using the paddle to turn the raft around and get a wider view.

They had been carried well away from the plane, now half-submerged. It would disappear soon. Gazing past Bari's head into the grey seascape, Noor caught no sight of ship or land. Still, such heavy rain might easily disguise land that was quite close.

Bari closed the flap again.

"No sign of land?" Noor said, hoping to be contradicted.

"No, but with a little luck we're near the Gulf Islands." He reached for the emergency pack again and pulled out a plastic-covered sheet of paper whose bold title read "Immediate Emergency Procedures."

Lightning flashed and flashed again, throwing an eerie orange glow over the interior, and making it hard for Noor's eyes to acclimatize. Bari frowned down at the paper for a moment, then lifted a hand to the centre of the canopy and turned on a little light.

Noor, uncomfortably curled in one corner, her shoulders resting against the edge of the raft, felt light-headed with the constant motion. Water was trickling down her back from her soaked hair. Her lacy stay-up stockings were slipping on her wet thighs, and she lifted a hand to strip them off as Bari pulled some rope and a curiously shaped piece of plastic out of the red sack.

"What's that for?" she asked, but he only shook his head as if her question were a bothersome fly. After a moment, her eyes fell on the wedding dress damply scrunched up under the satchel. It was slowly absorbing the water sloshing around the floor of the raft, but it was better than nothing. Noor reached out and pulled at the hem.

She knew she was being foolish and stupidly sentimental as she avoided using the beautiful overskirt and instead lifted one of the flounced underskirts and bent to wipe her face and hair on the impeccably handstitched silk. It came away blotched with black, green and tan, so no doubt her face was a mess. She tried wiping her hair and her arms, because she was starting to feel chilled, but the dress was too soaked to make any difference.

For several minutes as Bari got his bearings there was silence between them. Noor sat straighter and tried not to feel sick. Normally she was a good sailor. The raft was stamped with the information that it was for four, but it was a small enough space even for two when one of them was a runaway bride and the other her furious ex-bridegroom, she told herself with grim humour.

It was moving up and down with the stormy swell, the waves slapping it, the water on the floor sloshing around to produce deep discomfort. Once they felt a heave and a toss and then water pounded down on them, pushing at the canopy, and she knew a wave had washed right over them. The incessant drumming rain and the silence within made the little space even more claustrophobic.

Noor shivered. She had never been so close to the elements, so profoundly at their mercy.

And in this mood, that included Bari himself.

"How long do you think it will be before they find us?" she asked nervously.

Bari lifted an eyebrow and looked up from what he was reading.

"Who do you imagine will be looking?"

Five

There was a heartbeat of shocked silence. Thunder cracked and rolled again, but now, *Alhamdolillah,* it was moving off.

"What?" she whispered.

"Who knows we were on the plane? Who knows it went down?"

"But—radar!"

Bari shook his head. "We were probably flying underneath radar most of the time."

He began to unravel the sea anchor rope. "Even when people do discover that we went off in the plane, will there be any reason to assume that we have not arrived safely at our destination, whatever that might be?"

She stared at him. Did he really mean this might go on?

"Unless, of course, someone is expecting *you* somewhere." His eyes were hard as he spoke.

She didn't know what that meant. "What about our

hotel booking? Won't they ask questions when we don't turn up?"

A crack of laughter escaped him. "Who will be expecting us to take a honeymoon when we didn't get married?"

He went on with his task, as if he could forget from moment to moment that she was there. She hated that. Bari had never ignored her before, and although now she knew his intense interest had been an act, still she missed it.

She suddenly began to wonder what had happened after she ran. When had the alarm been raised? The guards at the gate must have noticed as she went roaring past in the bridal limousine, but what had they actually seen?

"Did people know what happened? Did they…" She faded off.

"Did they know my bride had changed her mind?" Bari supplied in harsh mockery, and abruptly the cool veneer dropped and his raw anger surged up again. "I don't know what they knew," he growled. "What does it matter? Insulting our families, our friends and all our guests! No reason on God's earth could justify such behaviour!"

No one ever criticized Noor, and in her current fragile state the stinging rebuke hit her hard.

"*You* were my reason!" she flared. "Easy for you to feel you should be allowed to walk all over me, but it's a bit much to expect me to agree!"

She was all the angrier, perhaps, because now that events had overtaken her, she was suddenly feeling very guilty. In countries like Bagestan and Barakat, hospitality was taken very seriously. It was practically a religious duty. And she had grown up in a family of exiles determined to maintain such traditions. It was in her blood almost as much as his.

"Walk all over you? Easier to walk over a bed of nails!" he snorted.

"With a soul as calloused as yours, no problem!"

"Not so calloused that I don't know when I've been lucky."

"Oh, I don't think so!" Noor snapped furiously. "A few minutes ago you were all for forcing me to the altar! Anyway, you weren't marrying me for my sweetness and light in the first place, were you? You had other mo—"

"Not even for your self-control under stress," he agreed. "Do you never consider pulling your own weight, Noor? Whatever *you* want is right?"

That was so outrageously unfair she gasped. "What do you know about it?" she demanded. "You've only known me for a few weeks! Ask my real friends if you want to know!"

Bari only shook his head and opened the hatch again. As more rain drove inside, he pushed something down into the water, then began playing out a line. Noor watched in silence. Not even for ready money would she now have offered her help. It would seem like giving in to his opinion of her, trying to win his favour. Not for a world!

But it irked her that he seemed not to have any expectation that she would be of help in what he was doing. Maybe he really did believe that she couldn't pull her weight; in any case, it seemed he could dismiss her completely from his field of consciousness.

She wished she could return the insult. She could probably have shared the raft with anyone else without feeling so claustrophobic; it was Bari's presence that made her feel so stifled.

The raft slowed and steadied somewhat as the little sea anchor took hold, and Bari closed the entrance again.

"Is there a first aid kit?" Noor asked, and Bari's piercing gaze fixed her.

"Where are you injured?"

"I only want the scissors."

"What for?" he demanded suspiciously.

"Life's not exciting enough, Bari. I'm going to punch a hole in the raft and add a bit of drama!" she snapped sarcastically, then held up one hand. "I broke my nails."

"The manicure will have to wait."

"I need to cut them off! They'll catch on everything!"

"You haven't lifted a finger so far, so what are they catching on?"

"You know what I mean."

"Other things have priority right now," he said with cold precision.

"Like what! Rowing to Australia?"

"You can start bailing." He tossed her yet another implement made of red plastic. "Use the observation hatch to get rid of the water."

Anything was better than sitting in sloshing water getting chilled, she supposed, but the bailer wasn't easy to use, and every time she put an arm out the hatch, water trickled down into her armpit, something that quickly became a form of Chinese torture.

Bari began to attach a plastic pouch to a narrow sleeve in the canopy above his head.

"What's that?" she asked warily, because she thought she knew.

"It collects rainwater."

Noor shook her head. "You're worried about conserving water?"

"The storm will pass. What then?"

Noor bit her lip and went on bailing.

When it was a little more than half full, Bari removed

the bag and tied the neck, setting it down. Then he picked up a plastic cup and began to help her bail. They worked together in silence for a time, bailing out as much as they could. Then they began sponging the floor dry.

"Do you think a boat or a plane will see us when the storm clears?"

"Not necessarily immediately."

"How long?"

He looked up from his task, as if exasperated that she insisted on forcing herself on his notice.

"You are not a fool, Noor! You know as well as I do that it is possible to be lost at sea for a very long time."

"But this is the Gulf of Barakat, not the Pacific!"

He apparently didn't consider that worth answering. She wondered whether they risked being carried out of the gulf and into the broader sea.

Abruptly she began to shiver. Her teeth chattered, and she realized how cold she had become. She wrapped her arms around herself, trying to stop the convulsions as shock suddenly began to make itself felt in her.

"I'm scared," she admitted in a whisper. "I'm so cold. Bari, would you—hold me?"

She despised herself for this show of weakness even as she asked.

Bari turned. His eyes fell on her bare foot, her ankle, then moved slowly up her brown calf to her bent knee. Then to the thin silk clinging to her body as snugly as a bathing suit. The teddy was made almost transparent by the wet, so that the nest of hair between her thighs was sharply revealed.

Just for a moment his eyes registered something very different than the bored irritation he had been treating her to. For one electric second they flashed with the familiar black fire that had so seduced her, and with an immediacy that was almost physical, Noor was remembering that other time they had been enclosed together in a storm....

They had sailed down the coast one morning and dropped anchor in a ruggedly scenic turquoise bay just before lunch. They swam in the crystal sea, over the submerged ruins of an ancient settlement that was now no more than a few squares outlined in raised earth and some scattered potsherds in the serene white sand, evidence of their kinship with those who had been drawn to this pleasant bay aeons ago.

Overlooking the bay, above on the rocky finger that marked the last reach of the Noor mountain range, was a more recent house in traditional Bagestani style. Its once-white paint was grey and peeling, its domed roof badly weather-damaged. A wooden door sagged on its hinges.

There were many such estates in Bagestan, she knew—abandoned by those who had fled the country under Ghasib's rule—including her family's own. Closer to the cities, such properties had mostly been expropriated by the government, but in remote areas often they had been left to the elements.

Noor had gazed up at the house as she swam in the jewelled water.

"So tragic," she said, for the house fired her imagination. "It must have been so beautiful, and now it looks—lonely. I wonder who it belongs to, and whether they intend to come back now and restore it."

Bari hadn't answered. Their bodies gleaming, they climbed back aboard and rinsed the salt off under the freshwater shower hose at the stern. Bari, the nozzle held above his head, suddenly pointed up at the sky. Dark clouds were moving out from behind the mountains.

"More rain," he said, with deeply felt satisfaction.

Then they sat under the yacht's shady awning, opened the picnic and spread out the little dishes of *bulghur* salad, *imam bayaldi, houmous* and a dozen other enticing concoctions.

The scent of richly spiced succulence rose delicately on the soft wind that blew over them, bringing the welcome rain clouds closer. Noor sighed luxuriously. She felt a sense of perfect physical well-being, bathed in a sensual glow that was the product of the heat, the sea, the food…and Bari's long muscled body, Bari's eyes.

He wanted her.

He had wanted her from the moment they met; he'd never tried to conceal that. That was why she had told him she was a virgin right at the beginning. She always told the men she dated, sooner or later, but with Bari it had to be sooner. *Only with my husband, or my future husband,* she'd said, the very first time he kissed her.

He had nodded, but she'd seen the muscle clench in his cheek, and his black eyes had burned hot enough to scorch her. And for the first time in such a situation she had felt the coil of something that might have been regret. For the first time she considered whether her friends—who talked about sex as if it were a great adventure to be undertaken with any man who looked like a promising travel companion—might be right.

Maybe he'd seen that momentary doubt. Something had flickered in his eyes then, as if he'd known he was the man who had the power to change her mind. Noor steeled herself to resist an onslaught, but in the days that followed Bari had never tried to wear her down, verbally or physically.

Other men had tried to undermine her, taking her to the brink and then insisting on her passion and their rights, but that treatment only fuelled her determination. Bari kissed her once, the kiss that so shifted her inner certainty that it had provoked her instant declaration of her status. After that, he hadn't kissed her, hadn't caressed her, hadn't complained…only his gaze had been given the freedom of her body. His eyes, not his mouth, had tasted the curving lips that had been made for kissing; his eyes had pierced her, as intimately as any thrust of his body, leaving her melting for more. His eyes, not his voice, told her what desire was in his blood.

She couldn't argue with a smile that faded and turned to a look of almost angry possession. She couldn't argue with the tightening of the generous mouth, the clenching of his strong, dark fist as he struggled against passion. And she couldn't resist when he insisted on seeing her, day after day, though it was an unnamed torment to them both.

She told herself his self-control was a relief to her, that she was glad his powerful desire didn't lead him to try to undermine her resolve. But in the long, hot Eastern nights, when she awoke in her solitary bed remembering Bari's eyes in lamplight, or the touch of his hand as it guided her and then lifted from her skin, slowly, weighted by deep reluctance, when her body was filled with yearning and a betraying wish that he had not lifted his hand, but had tightened his hold, had insisted on possession, was here beside her in the bed, to reach for and embrace—then what she felt was something that was almost regret.

The breeze grew stronger under the shadow of the awning, and brushed her forehead with the cool promise of rain.

"Do you think the drought is really over?" she asked. It had already rained twice in two days, and the whole country was rejoicing as if this relief, too, could be laid at the new Sultan's door.

He looked at her. "Yes," he said, his voice creating another sensation on her skin. "The drought is over. It has been long, yes? Too long."

There was a silence as she pretended not to understand him.

"Are you hungry, Noor?"

Noor nodded wordlessly and reached out at random to spoon something luscious onto her plate. Bari tore a piece of bread from the small, tender loaf in front of him, dipped it in spiced olive oil, lifted his chin and slipped the melting morsel between his lips.

Hunger, not for food, whipped her with a ferocity born of the long days and nights of unsatisfied desire. Days and nights when he had given her everything to build her hunger, and nothing against which to sharpen her resistance.

A smudge of oil glazed his lower lip. His upper lip pressed down to suck it off, and his eyes caught her gaze as his lips relaxed again into sensual fullness.

He lowered his lids and reached for the bread. His palm cupped and accommodated to the breastlike roundness of the loaf with deeply sensual appreciation, his long, square fingers dark against the whiteness of the loaf, sure and competent. He offered Noor a torn chunk of bread.

Her fingertips brushed his knuckles, and she winced as her wrist went weak. The little chunk of bread fell on the table between them. Noor breathed in, her eyes rising irresistibly to meet his gaze. He knew. Of course he knew. She swallowed, licked her dry lips.

"Thank you," she murmured, reaching for the bread again.

There was cutlery in the picnic basket, but Bari ate using his fingers or bread as his only tools. Somehow, she didn't know how, this added to the sensual impact of the moment. Then she realized that it was because he was a sensualist. Bari ate with his hands because the sensation of touch added to his pleasure in the food.

Just so, a part of her whispered, would he take pleasure in her body, if she allowed it. Touch, taste, scent…he gloried in his senses, and his senses would glory in her flesh.

He lifted a piece of chicken and tore it apart, offering her a morsel from fingers slippery with melted butter and olive oil, then watched in appreciation as her white teeth closed on the tidbit. He grunted when her lips brushed his skin and, in half-involuntary mimicry of his sensual approach, she closed her lips around his fingertip and sucked the spiced oil from his slightly raspy skin.

A bolt of electricity shot through her, all the way to her toes. Her eyes lifted as if he forced them up to lock with his gaze.

She was on very dangerous ground, but a treacherous part of her, the part that wanted to give in, kept telling her that nothing had happened. He hadn't even kissed her, let alone got close to making love. They were only eating.

But another part of her knew that Bari wasn't like other men, and that this attraction was like nothing she'd ever felt before, and that the point of no return was almost upon her.

The hungry part, the part that was desperate to experience Bari's sensuality at the deepest level, won out, and in involuntary temptation she licked her lips and smiled.

His eyelids drooped, and a possessive gleam shot out from under the lowered lids to tell her that she was lost. He scooped up another morsel of food and fed it to her with one hand, while the other tenderly stroked her throat and chin.

Her skin ignited like dry brush at a lightning strike. Noor opened her eyes and her mouth, but though his face was so close, he did not kiss her.

A delicate assault on her senses began. Resting his elbows on the table, Bari leaned forward to murmur in her ear that she was beautiful, desirable, and that no man could see her and not want her. Then he made her drink from his glass. Like a child—but not like a child.

He stroked her neck, her shoulder above the pretty gauzy sarong she had tied over her bathing suit, her hand, her wrist. He poured wine into her cupped hand and sucked it out with a sexual need that she felt as a blow. He explored her palm with his tongue and lips as if she, too, were heady wine.

As they ate, one desire was sated, but another grew. She felt her body's need for him hammer its urgent message in her blood, her brain, her skin, her breasts, her abdomen. His need for her was in his lips, his tongue, his trembling hands, and in his dark, approving eyes.

Meanwhile, across the sky, dark clouds were massing and moving closer. A rumble of thunder breached the silence now and then, and warm wind whipped at the canvas canopy that protected them from the sun. She felt that her body was like the parched earth that had longed for the sky's blessing for long months and years, and now that he was near it would be sin and worse than sin to turn away into dryness and infertility again.

Down inside the cabin there was a stateroom, and a bed. After an endless time, Bari drew her up from her seat and led her there, pushing her down onto the soft cushions and following to stretch his hungry body out beside her. Then he took her ruthlessly into his arms and, for the first time, let slip the tight rein he had kept on his passion....

Something landed in her lap, bringing her out of her reverie. She blushed, as if Bari might have guessed her thoughts.

"And what's this?" She lifted the little plastic envelope. She was shivering in earnest now.

"A foil blanket. It is dangerous to attempt buddy warmth with only two people in a four-man raft," Bari said. "All the weight in one place could destabilize the raft."

His voice was so full of contemptuous dismissal that she burned with embarrassment, as if she *had* been offering him sex and been rejected.

She didn't believe what he had just said. He simply didn't want to touch her. The rage and hurt of this morning's discovery flooded her mind once more. She was in a ferment to shake him out of his damned supercilious contempt, his smug calm.

"What gives you the right to look at me as if—as if…I was asking for *comfort!*" she shouted. "When did I *ever* throw myself at you? You were the one! Right from the beginning—as if I were water in the desert!"

Tears stung her eyes, but she would *not* be so weak!

"Instead you were a mirage," Bari said harshly, as her emotions succeeded in igniting his own.

"Me?" she exclaimed, choking on the injustice. "*I* wasn't the mirage! *I* never lied!"

"What was it when you said you would marry me, if not a lie?"

His voice was cold with fury. In the red glow cast by the canopy he looked unfamiliar, an angry stranger.

And that was what he was. She didn't know him at all.

"What was it when *you* said you wanted to marry me?" she countered hotly, the pent-up words bursting from her. "You don't want to marry me, and never did! And before you deny it, I overheard your aunt and your cousin talking. You're only marrying me because your grandfather wants an alliance with his old friend's family. He ordered you to marry me, and you were furious about it. You have to marry me to inherit the family property, isn't that right? You don't love me!"

He watched her steadily, one eyebrow lifted.

"Do you!" she prodded. *"Do you!"*

"No, Noor," Bari replied in a slow, calm voice, not at all the voice of a man caught out. "No, I don't love you. Why are you pretending outrage when you have always known it?"

Six

Noor's mouth opened in slow, appalled disbelief, but Bari gave no quarter.

"I never told you I loved you. You didn't ask to hear it. What you wanted was a wealthy, socially connected man who would cater to your desire for a life of selfish pleasure. That was what I offered you. That was your price, Noor."

"My *price!*"

"So the discovery that you say you have now made—that love is not part of our bargain—will not serve as an excuse. I ask you again—why did you back out of the agreement that both of us understood from the beginning? And why did you choose such a moment, such a grotesque and offensive way to do it?"

His teeth and eyes flashed in an angry smile.

"It's not true!" she cried, but if he heard the dismay in her voice it left him unmoved.

"What is not true? What part of what I have said do you dispute?"

"If you didn't love me, why didn't you tell me that when you proposed?"

"You never asked. My reasons for wishing the marriage formed no part of our bargain. You could have made it so, but you did not choose to know."

"Only because I thought—I thought—"

"What did you think?" His eyes narrowed. "You thought I loved you?" Fierce laughter erupted from him. "You got it all, is that what you thought, Noor? I offered you wealth and social connections, and my family's honour, and now you say you thought you had my love, too—and what were you offering in exchange? Not love, for you love only yourself."

"That's not true!" she cried, stunned by this battering. "Anyway, I didn't need your wealth or social conn—"

"Your name, that was the sum total of what you brought to our agreement. That you are the descendant of a man my grandfather remembers with love and respect."

His voice dripped with bitterness, and she knew then without a doubt that what she had overheard his cousin and aunt saying was the truth. He had been brutally angry over his grandfather's decision.

"Why do you flinch from admitting it?"

She could feel tears burning her eyes, but not for the world would she let Bari see how affected she was, her skin crawling with humiliation and shame.

"You pretended!" she accused him, her voice hovering on a sob. "Try and deny that! Don't call me a fool when you know perfectly well you acted as if you were besotted with me!"

He lifted a hand, a shoulder, in an expressive shrug. "You are a sexually attractive woman. But if you had really wanted my love, Noor, you would have acted like a woman who wants to be loved, not like one who knows she can do no wrong. When did you concern yourself with my good opinion? With the regard of my mother and sisters? With anyone's well-being but your own? Nothing is as important to you as your own wishes, it seems. Whose opinion matters to you? Whose feelings do you consider?"

"That's a lie!"

"So sure are you of your worth that you didn't notice I never spoke of love! Yet—you tell me now—all the time you were assuming that I loved you passionately. Is that the attitude of a woman with a heart? To take love for granted?

"And if you had ever believed you loved me, you would have told me so. Even when there is nothing but sex a woman will say *I love you*. But not you. *Oh, Bari, isn't it wonderful!* That is what you said. But no word of love."

Anger and humiliation scorched her. She had never been so insulted, so bitterly condemned.

"I was a virgin! Why do you think I waited all that time, if not for love?"

He smiled. "You waited for a husband. You said to me, *only with my husband, or my future husband,* not *only with the man I love.*"

"It went without saying. Of course I expected to love the man I married!"

His black eyes fixed her, as if with pins to a board. "And did you love him, the man you nearly married?" Her heart fluttered a protest.

"I—" Her mind seemed to stumble.

"Go on, Noor. Tell me you love me," Bari challenged mockingly.

Was he right? Was it the image she had loved, and not the man at all? What was love? She hesitated, and he laughed outright.

"You can't expect me to say it *now!*" she cried.

"If you imagine love is so easily killed, then you know nothing of love. You are suffering from bruised pride, and you imagine you have been crossed in love!"

"That is so untrue!"

He eyed her coldly. "And is this truly why you ran from our wedding ceremony minutes before it was to begin, leaving all our guests, without a word of explanation to them or to our families or to me? Because of an insult to your pride? Because of a conversation you overheard?"

Noor could hardly take it in. How could he be throwing her accusation back in her face like this? She had been on a rock, and with a wave of words he had changed that into shifting sand.

This isn't really happening! her brain kept insisting. *This is a dream!*

How had she gone from being an excited, beautiful bride, wearing the most exquisite dress in the world and a diamond worth a sultan's ransom, waiting for her wedding to a man who was crazy for her, to this—having flown through a terrifying storm in fear for her life, and crash-landed at sea, she was now lying in a storm-tossed life raft waiting for rescue that might not come, her makeup streaked, her nails broken and torn, her hair in rat's tails, wet, naked and shivering, and squashed into a tiny space with that same man who now despised her?

But worst of all was what she was hearing about herself. Did she act like a woman so used to being loved she took it for granted?

It wasn't true. If she had believed Bari loved her it

was because of the way he had treated her, not because that was her first assumption.

"I don't take love for granted!" Noor felt another chill sweep through her and, suddenly reminded, she sat up and tore the plastic bag from the tiny packet he had thrown her. She unfurled a sheet of rustling gold foil that glowed and glittered even in the dimness.

"Silver side in for warmth," Bari said, and began working a small air pump.

She wrapped herself in it. Whatever the strange foil was, it had an immediate effect on her chill. But it offered poor protection against Bari's accusations. They had already hit home.

"It looks like the Sultana's robes at the coronation," she muttered, tweaking the folds around her, trying to dispel her own gloom, trying to prevent herself hearing what he had said, what he really thought of her.

Could it be true? People had always loved her. Everyone she knew loved her. And not just her mother and father and her brothers and Jalia and her friends. At school she had been popular with everyone—except for a few girls who were jealous, she amended carefully…but no one was loved by everybody in the world! You couldn't be human and not have *some* enemies! Some girls were jealous of her because her family spoiled her, she'd always known that. She'd had lots of spending money and the freedom to do what she liked, and of course people hated that….

Bari's family had been cool with her, some of them. But she couldn't have cared less what they thought of her. Why should she? Bari was right about that—she'd taken no trouble to make them like her, not Noor! If they didn't like her as she was, that was their problem. Anyway, she'd told herself, it was only jealousy because Bari had fallen for her so hard.

But if it turned out Bari hadn't fallen for her, and they knew it, what did that mean?

That they disliked her for herself?

What had she ever done to deserve dislike? When had she ever hurt anyone?

As if in answer, her brain suddenly conjured up the scene her flight must have created. Jalia and the brides-maids coming to the door of her bedroom, one of the women going to the bathroom to call her…had they gone searching through the house? And when she was nowhere to be found—what would they have thought? Her parents—what had they imagined? What were they going through now?

She thought of the guests, and what bewilderment they must have felt—were probably still feeling. What she had done was a personal insult to them all. She had treated them as if they didn't matter in the least. Bari was right—she had thought her own concerns of over-riding importance. Some of their guests had flown half-way around the world to celebrate with her, and she hadn't even done them the simple honour of telling them that she had changed her mind and the wedding wouldn't take place.

As if that understanding unlocked a door in her heart, a host of other visions suddenly flashed through her un-willing mind, one after the other. Moments in her past when she had acted selfishly, even cruelly. Girls at school whom she had cut, or insulted, or laughed at when they tried to be popular, or wore the wrong clothes. Friends she had dropped without explanation, a boy she had mocked when he asked her out…

All the time believing she was in the right. Noor

Ashkani could do no wrong. She brooked no criticism. Dare to doubt Noor's actions and you were out of the charmed circle before you took another breath.

All her life she had acted as if she were the person who mattered. She hadn't believed that consciously, but she could see with painful clarity now that it had been the unconscious basis of her actions.

The discovery that Bari didn't love her had cut to the quick her self-importance, and she had reacted with pure arrogance. She had hurt and insulted everyone.

Noor looked up. Bari's expression was grim, but even if it hadn't been, she couldn't tell him what thoughts and what painful self-realization poured through her. Not Bari, of all people, who sat in such harsh judgement and had never loved—probably didn't even like—her.

Bari watched his bride impassively, her chin trembling as she struggled against emotion. She sat with head bent, her hands hiding her face, tears trickling down her cheeks. He let her cry for a few minutes. It was probably no more than the shock of the crash being released, and he was angry enough to remain unmoved. But when the choked sobs began to become a wail, it was time to call a halt.

"That's enough," he ordered without apology, tossing another packet at her. It landed on the rustling gold blanket. "You can't afford to waste any more energy."

Noor's breathing shifted into a series of panting gasps, like a child, as she struggled to stifle her tears. She wiped her face and blew her nose on her beautiful dress, picked up the little plastic box and gazed at it stupidly.

"What is it?"

"First aid kit," he said.

Why had she asked for the kit? The mixture of shame

and misery kept her head bent, and she found relief in wrestling with the plastic seal. She reached for the flashlight and shone it briefly on the contents. The first thing her eyes fell on was a vial of seasickness pills.

As if there were a direct causal link, Noor's stomach heaved. With a strangled cry she tossed the kit and the flashlight aside and dived for the entrance, her gold foil cloak rustling wildly. She ripped the flap down and, thrusting her head out into the storm, clutched the side of the raft, leaned over, and heaved up the shock and grief and shame and the million other undefined things she was feeling, until there seemed to be nothing left, either in her stomach or in her heart.

When it was over at last, she reached her hand down into the sea and scooped up handfuls of water to wash her face and rinse her mouth. The salt stung her eyes and tasted on her lips, but the coolness of the water seemed to bring her back to herself.

When she was through she felt purged, cleansed. She drew her head back inside and sealed the flap again. Bari ignored her.

Well, she wasn't asking for his sympathy. She wasn't asking for anything from him. She had learned something about herself in the past half hour, and it had been a very painful lesson. Some fundamental shift seemed to have happened in her, and for the second time in a few months she had the sensation of not knowing who she was.

But there was no way she was going to try to tell Bari that. He would probably think she was making it up.

"The storm is passing," she said, wrapping herself securely in the rustling golden foil again. "I think I saw land."

He nodded without looking up. He was still working the air pump, and the floor was slowly inflating.

"May I have a drink of water?"

He tossed her the little plastic cup he had been bailing with. "Catch some rainwater in that."

Noor bit back an indignant response. She supposed his caution was appropriate, even praiseworthy—if they were going to be lost for any length of time the water conservation started now, even if that was land she had seen.

But he could have been less rude about it.

"I see we aren't going to be bound by any silly code of polite conduct while we're stuck here," she rashly remarked.

Leaving herself wide open, of course, and she realized it as soon as it was too late to call the comment back. Bari lifted an eyebrow, and though his face was in shadow, she could guess the expression in his eyes.

"You are speaking, of course, as someone who isn't bound by any code of conduct at any time."

There was no winning that one. Noor lifted the cup up to the sleeve as she had seen him do, but he had pushed it inside out. She fiddled with it for a moment, without discovering the trick. She glanced over at Bari, but he was working the air pump, his head bent.

Fine! She wasn't nearly as helpless or stupid as he obviously believed, and she'd be *damned* if she would ask for his help!

After a few moments she was rewarded with the sound of water dripping into the cup. *Nyaaa,* she told him in her head, but not by so much as the tip of her tongue did she let him see her triumph.

The rain funnelled down more slowly than before, and she suddenly realized how the rain had slackened, and how far away the thunder was. She filled the cup three times and drank the curiously tasteless liquid, then glanced at Bari.

"Do you want a drink?"

He looked up, surprised. "Yes, thanks."

Noor bit back a resentful remark—did he really think she was incapable of putting herself out for someone else even in a situation like this?—and passed the filled cup to him without comment. He tossed off the water in one gulp and gave it back to her with a murmur of thanks. She filled it again, and he drank again.

The transaction felt strange and awkward to her, because she felt uncomfortable with him now. No doubt Bari would say it was because she was so unused to doing even the simplest things for other people. But what did he know about her?

"I suppose it has never occurred to you," she remarked to the cup as she filled it for him for the third time, "that you have seen me in a very limited set of circumstances—namely, when I was (a) effectively on holiday, (b) had just learned, among other things, that my family owned a *palace* and (c) was suddenly being treated as a princess by everyone around me? How many people you know would have kept their heads in a situation like mine?"

Her eyes met his as she passed him the cup again. "You think a person should not be judged by their behaviour when life is going well for them?"

"Welcome to The Kangaroo Courtroom of the Waves," Noor announced bitterly. "Forget I spoke."

Bari drank and handed her the empty cup, signalling that he didn't want any more. Noor filled the cup one last time and then picked up the pack of seasickness pills and pressed one out into her palm.

Her broken fingernail caught as she did so, and after swallowing the pill she reached for the first aid kit again, located the scissors, and cut the three torn nails off short, as neatly as she could. She spread out her hands. If her nails were going to keep on breaking at the current rate it would be smarter to cut them all down now. On the other hand, if rescue were near…

Something made her lift her eyes, and she found Bari watching her, a cynical gleam in his gaze.

"Look on the bright side—they may have time to regrow before you have to face your admiring public again," he said.

Gritting her teeth, Noor picked up the scissors again and one by one cut the rest of her nails short.

"I hope you aren't making a mistake. Nails like that might have come in handy. Who knows how many fish we may need to scale, for example?"

Noor gave him back look for look. "No worries. I'm sure your ceremonial sword will do the job. It'll be a comfort to you to know all that family history is useful for something."

And so the battle lines were drawn.

Seven

Noor cast a half-despairing look around as they approached land. The faint shape she had seen earlier had proved to be a small, isolated island, probably somewhere on the outer fringes of the Gulf Island group.

The clouds had given way to blazing sunshine, which quickly turned the life raft into a sauna. But the sun's heat was fading now as it neared the horizon, and Noor was wondering whether it was safe to emerge.

Bari was sitting out on the edge of the raft using one of the paddles as a makeshift rudder, keeping the raft on a heading towards the island. He was also trailing a fishing line.

He had stripped off the purple silk jacket and was wearing it on his head, the sleeves twisted into rope and tied around his forehead, to form a makeshift keffiyeh. Anyone else, Noor reflected bitterly, would have looked like a complete idiot. Bari looked like a genie in a fairy tale, skin bronzed, chest and arm muscles rippling, white silk *shalwar* enfolding his legs, bare feet. He seemed perfectly at home.

Noor, on the other hand, had been forced by the fierce sun to stay inside the stifling confines of the raft through the worst heat of the day, painstakingly cutting a sarong and a scarf from the wet skirt of her wedding dress with scissors that weren't up to the job. Without such protection she couldn't hope to face the sun. Her predicament hadn't been helped by Bari's insistence that they had had plenty of water to get them through the first twenty-four hours.

They were communicating in monosyllables.

The island itself was a relatively attractive prospect, with a small curving bay protected by a rocky outcrop at one end, and clustered palm trees that promised water. But Noor had stopped hoping some time ago that it might also hold the Gulf Eden Resort.

Deciding that the sun had lost its danger, she carefully slipped up through the canopy entrance with the wet scarf in her hand, and as she did so, she was struck by a sudden, unconnected thought.

"Wait a minute!" she exclaimed, breaking the hostile silence unthinkingly. "Isn't a radio beacon part of the emergency equipment of this raft? An EPIRB?"

Bari looked at her.

She urged excitedly, "I'm sure my friends all have it as part of their yacht emergency kit."

"It isn't a part of the standard raft emergency kit. There was one aboard the plane…." He pressed his lips together in mute resignation.

Noor moaned her despair. "Oh, God, you *forgot* it?"

As if to comfort her, Bari said, "We have flares. When it is dark we will set one off."

"Why don't we do it now? Flares are visible in daylight, aren't they?"

"Is it worth wasting a flare merely to ease the present tedium?"

Noor wasn't used to the feeling that someone was secretly laughing at her, and she didn't like it. She held up the damp silk, and felt cooler just watching it flap in the breeze.

"It would be nice to see some action around here, and you don't seem to be having much luck with the fish," she said waspishly. "Why do you talk of wasting them? How many are there?"

"Two."

"Is that all? What if no one sees them? Oh, my God, and it's such a small island, too! Don't you think it might be better to stay in the raft in the hopes of reaching an island where there's more chance of finding people?"

Bari looked up, and his breath caught on a hiss which she did not hear. Standing in the entrance opening opposite him, Noor was leaning lightly back on the canopy, one foot propped on the edge of the raft, the square of silk forgotten in her hand. Her head tilted back while she turned her face this way and that under the luxurious caress of the wind.

Just so had she moved under the stroking of his lips.

Her body was barely covered by the delicate garment she wore, which did nothing to hide that creamy skin, warm with a light tan everywhere except her breasts and abdomen, the paler-textured places he knew as well as his own hand, even after only one interlude of lovemaking.

Her hair was damp with sweat at her temples, as if he had just made love to her. Her breasts swelled with the movement of her arms, pressing against the soft, expensive lace that cupped them.

The top of her thighs, with the thin damp silk revealing the nest of hair, was right in his line of vision. All
he had to do was bend forward to bury his mouth where
his eyes were. Heavy sensual memory tugged at his
limbs, asking to be repeated. The hard tension of his
body urged him.

"Wouldn't it be better?" Noor's impatient voice
brought him back to the question. More hope of finding other people, was that what she wanted? Bari's jaw
tightened in a grim smile.

"Does the thought of being without your entourage
so terrify you?"

"My *entourage?*"

"You are afraid that you can't live without the
army of doting servants and friends and Jalia and your
brothers—or at least someone who might be willing to
replace them? You would prefer to remain in the raft,
with whatever dangers that entails, than face the possibility that you will now have to fend for yourself?"

His tone suggested that another minute on the raft
with her would drive him to suicide. His teeth flashed
in the mocking smile that her lacerated spirit suddenly
found too familiar. Had the smiles that had melted her
bones always secretly mocked her?

Noor gritted her teeth.

"I would prefer to take the rational course of action,
regardless of my more immediate feelings," she said, her
jaw tight. "But I see that in a fifty-fifty disagreement between brains and brawn, brawn is always going to get
its way!"

His smile didn't falter, though his eyes flashed a
message that raised nervous goose bumps on her arms.
"Alas, it is the story of your sex," he mocked. "Always
right, and always powerless."

It was a relief to be speaking in whole sentences again, whatever the sentiments being expressed. Feeling had to come out somehow, Noor felt, or eat her alive.

"Not *always* powerless," she snapped. "The patriarchy has had a brief reign, really—a mere two or three thousand years. A hiccup of deviance in the natural order."

"And are you expecting the return of the all-wise matriarchy any time soon?"

"Well, it'll be either that or the complete destruction of the species, won't it?" Noor snapped.

"You think men are certain to lead the world to destruction?"

"I think men who fear and hate women and don't allow us a voice or listen to our wisdom have brought us to the brink of it already. Tell me I'm wrong!"

"And you include me in their numbers," Bari said flatly. "How typical of a woman who has heard criticism of herself, to expand that into a generalized misogyny in the soul of the speaker!"

She bent over, bringing her face on a level with his.

"I don't give a damn about your criticism or dislike of me!" she lied fiercely, feeling that his black eyes burned her more harshly than the sun. "What I do care about is your assumption that my query over whether we should land on this particular island should be mocked, rather than taken into rational consideration, because it disagrees with *your* all-seeing, all-knowing decision on the matter! What makes you such a bloody expert on shipwreck? Ever done it before? Neither have I! That makes us equals in this situation, I think. Except that I need your agreement to go on sailing, and you don't need mine to land. Or should I push you overboard and steer the thing myself?"

"By all means, if you think you can."

"So here we are back at brains and brawn again. See?" Noor held up her hands and smiled, as if a slow pupil had finally been led to the light. Her smile was bright and mocking, and she could see it got under his skin in spite of his intentions.

She tried not to feel that she was lighting a fuse on an unknown quantity of explosive.

"Don't be so quick to assign yourself *all* the brains. I've told you before that these islands are now uninhabited. Except for the Gulf Eden Resort. Even a woman, I think, should have doubts about her ability to find one particular island when she doesn't know its position or her own."

Noor gritted her teeth. "No wonder men are turning the world into such a hell!" she said feebly. It was the only riposte she could think of.

"And when women ruled the world, everyone lived in paradise?"

"You don't find any city walls in the ancient matriarchal societies, do you?" Noor pointed out. "Sumer—"

"I suppose you learned this nonsense in *Feminist Perspectives on History for Beginners!*" Bari interrupted with harsh irony. "You don't find any city walls around Persepolis, either. The capital of the Persian Empire, which was ruled by the Achaemenid *kings*. It spread to become the greatest empire in antiquity. Are you suggesting it was not militaristic?"

"Tell me, is it nonsense because it's feminist, or because the ideas expressed are not your own?" Noor asked sweetly.

But the mocking tone didn't disguise her real feelings from herself. She glared down into his face, and noted helplessly how the sinking sun melted in his dark eyes, glowed on the black curls that clustered over his head.

The sea, too, was glittering with its rich golden light. The sapphire and amethyst of the deeper sea had given way now to turquoise and emerald, with flashes of white gold. It was as if some celestial painter had brushed diamonds on the crest of every ripple of the sea, as on each coal-black curl, underlining Bari's vital connection with the rest of creation, and reminding her of that other time they had drifted on the waves as the sun set. Then his hand had never been far from her skin, stroking her in tender possession in the aftermath of their lovemaking—her breast, her arm, her flank.

Her heart beat hard. So he was handsome, so what? So he had made the kind of love to her you read about in books! How could she be so weak as to find him attractive now that she knew what she knew?

And he was perfectly right: she didn't love him, and never had.

Meanwhile, Bari damped down his anger, though it cost him a struggle. He knew it would be dangerous to allow anger—or any emotion—to overwhelm him in these circumstances.

"It is because such ideas are based on nothing," he replied levelly. "We can scarcely hope to understand our neighbours today. How do we dream that we know anything of how societies operated thousands of years ago?"

Under the water now a floor of white sand appeared, across which their shadow rose and fell with the waves. Noor watched a school of delicate, sinuous, silver-and-turquoise fish flee from the threatening shape as the raft approached.

Suddenly Bari's fishing line jerked tight, and their conversation, such as it was, dissolved. Bari picked up the bailer and thrust it at Noor with a brief "Hold that and try to get it under him!" Then his strong hands began to pull the line with slow careful pressure, drawing the struggling fish closer and closer, playing it a little, and then inexorably drawing it in again.

Their differences were forgotten as they worked together on the urgent task of bringing in tonight's dinner, and when the fish had been captured, they smiled at each other involuntarily, forgetting their conflict for the moment.

"I could almost eat it raw!" she cried.

"You might have to."

The raft was being carried at an angle away from the sandy part of the beach towards the rocks. Bari jumped out, landed in waist-deep water and, waving her to stay aboard, dragged the painter over his shoulder. His arm and back muscles rippled as he guided the little raft into the long shadow of a rugged outcrop of black rock that thrust up out of the smooth white sand, the sea splashing gently against it.

Noor watched in helpless fascination as he strode up the sloping beach, the water level dropping to reveal his slim waist, his muscled hips, strong thighs. The white cloth of his *shalwar,* stained dark by the water, clung to him, outlining every rippling fold of well-toned muscle. The inside of her own thighs unexpectedly melted at the sudden sense-memory of the firmness of his body against her in those pleasure-drugged minutes when her legs had clung to him and he moved inside her.

It had been painful and an utter delight all at once, as her body now insistently reminded her. The slap of the waves against the raft, its gentle rise and fall, the erotic swelling that lifted the raft and let it sink, all conspired to bring back her first experience of that primal motion, that fundamental rhythm underlying all creation.

Though she hadn't achieved the peak under the thrust of his body, the pain of lost virginity hadn't stopped her hunger for him, for more, more, more. His mouth and his hands had been what sent her over the edge into swooping pleasure, but it wasn't mouth and hands she remembered now. It was him deep inside her, pushing her towards some magical truth that had eluded her then but still magnetically beckoned and promised. The mere touch of him had given her a deep satisfaction, even without the soaring pleasure, and it was that which, to her horror, she was suddenly yearning and aching for.

The completion. The sense of connection at the deepest level. The oneness of it.

He was despising you all the time, Noor reminded herself fiercely. *It was an act to trick you. He was prostituting himself for his grandfather's money.*

The life raft ran aground, and she climbed out of it with a slight stagger. The waves bubbled and frothed against her shins, warm and inviting.

"We must carry it ashore. Take that side," Bari commanded, as if he expected to be obeyed, and Noor just couldn't think of a way to rebel that wouldn't end with her having to obey. When they had carried the raft above the high-tide mark and into the lee of the rock, he nodded approvingly, as if to a child.

"Very good."

He searched inside for the flashlight, and Noor turned away from the sight of him to watch the sun set underneath a perfect spectrum of colours: blood-red at the horizon, then glowing orange, golden yellow, soft green blending to blue, then through deeper and deeper blues to indigo and finally, overhead, to dark amethyst.

Underneath the sky the water reflected the sparkling,

deep velvet blackness, the surface glowing with dancing touches of red and gold.

"Princess!" The voice broke in to her reverie and she looked up to see the mocking grin she so hated.

"I thought so!" Bari said, grinning. "But there's no *princess* on this island, Princess. The title's temporarily suspended. Everybody pulls their own weight here."

Noor glared at him. "I was just watching the sunset for a moment!" She didn't add, *as a way of keeping my eyes off your butt.* It would be a cold day in hell before she said anything like that.

"Uh-huh," Bari said, as if he didn't believe a word of it. "Well, sunset is the last thing you have time for, Princess. If you want to eat, you're going to have to work for it."

"I don't think it's so urgent we can't take a moment to get our bearings!"

"The sun's setting fast. Get your bearings in the morning. You can start by collecting stones to circle the fire. Then gut the fish."

"And what will you be doing while I do all that?" Noor enquired gently.

"Gathering firewood, Princess," he informed her, as if he'd been hoping she would ask. "Unless you were serious about eating your dinner raw."

He lifted his hand and dropped it again, and with a tiny chunk of sound, a knife embedded itself in the sand at her feet.

In the gathering darkness, Noor collected stones and laid them in a circle to contain their fire. Then she stood and looked around. In among the trees the beam of Bari's flashlight flicked up and down.

Strange places could be frightening at the best of times. She shivered, and felt how naked and unprotected she was with only the homemade sarong to cover her. She was glad he meant to make a fire.

If she had never gutted a fish before, at least she had seen it done often enough to make a reasonable stab at the process. Bari was probably hoping she would balk at the task, and she was determined to disappoint him. So Noor took a deep breath, picked up the knife, and with a little moue slit the still-graceful silver-grey body and cleaned it. She was laying the fish on a palm leaf when Bari returned with his arms full.

"Good girl, Princess!" he applauded, eyeing her preparations.

Noor gritted her teeth. "Good boy, Sheikh!" she said.

His eyelids drooped.

"Who started it?" she demanded, preempting any complaint.

Bari laughed. Noor went down to the sea to rinse her hands. When she returned, Bari had laid a fire and was carefully lighting it. At his command, she went to get the bag of water and the little plastic cup out of the raft. She picked up the foil sheet and dragged it around her shoulders, then opened another and laid it down as a picnic blanket—but there the comparison ended. There was nothing else to set out, no other preparation she could make. They had no utensils, no plates, no salt, nothing.

Noor wrapped the thin foil around her against the increasing chill, and held the feeling of panic at bay. They were lucky, she told herself firmly. Bari had been right—they were a thousand times safer on dry land than lost at sea on a tiny raft.

The last rays of the sun faded and darkness swept over them, broken only by the flickering blaze of their tiny campfire. In the darkness the silence was intense.

The rushing of the sea, the crackling of the burning wood, the cry of an unknown bird or animal in the deeper shadows of the trees, against that backdrop of silence, only told them of their aloneness.

Eight

Late in the night Bari lay awake, listening to his bride's soft breathing beside him as if it were the wind of his soul. Overhead, beyond the swathe of wedding veil that protected them, moon and stars glowed too brightly in the purple-black sky. At his feet, the sea slapped and shushed, its deep, living black painted with thick gold light. There was no horizon; he was caught in a web of spangled blackness that had neither beginning nor end.

Emotionally, too, he was caught in a web.

No, Noor, I don't love you.

That his grandfather should try to dictate Bari's choice of wife was one thing. He was an old man. Of course he expected to rule his family's fortunes in the old way, the way of generations before him. And of course nostalgia had a strong hold on his imagination.

The timing of the demand, however, was a cause almost for outrage. It was evidence of how badly Jabir al

Khalid was losing his grip that his first act, in the face of the monumental difficulties and the dedicated work that would necessarily follow the astonishing achievement of the Return, had been to track down the family of his old friend Faruq Durrani in the hopes of arranging a marriage for his grandson.

Marriage was the last thing on Bari's agenda. What time had he for the courtship and wooing that a woman had a right to expect, even in an arranged marriage? He had urgent tasks ahead of him, both as Cup Companion to a Sultan endeavouring to make an effective transition to a new order, and as the heir to the neglected family interests in Bagestan.

But his grandfather had insisted, even when Faruq Durrani's most eligible granddaughter proved to be a foreigner, born and raised in the West, into wealth and privilege without responsibility, who was very unlikely to be suited to joining Bari in his life's work.

And doubtless, Bari had pointed out to his grandfather with as much patience as he could muster, a woman who would be impatient with any attempt to arrange a marriage. As a Westerner, she would feel it her right to fall in love with a man of her own choosing, to be courted "for herself."

The old man had understood that modern concept. He had ordered that there should be no conventional overtures for an arranged marriage—no, Bari would have to woo and win the girl.

All that was bad enough, but much worse was to come. Before Bari could refuse this mad request outright, Jabir al Khalid delivered his ultimatum.

The blackmail had shocked them all. It told Bari that his grandfather was well aware that times had changed. He knew that his word was no longer law. He was not powerful in the way of his father and his father's fathers. So he was making up for the lack of moral power with threat—marry this woman or watch the family estates fall into further disrepair as cousins vie to win the prize. Never set foot on al Khalid property except as a guest of someone who cares nothing for its heritage.

The old man also knew—no one better—that his grandson had always dreamed of returning to Bagestan when it was liberated. Bari had worked with Ashraf Durrani throughout his determined, dangerous bid to restore the al Jawadis to the throne, and he intended and expected to stay and help to rebuild the country and his own family's heritage when that bid was successful.

But when the joy of the people was still ringing in their ears, when Bari might have expected congratulations from his grandfather, who had wanted nothing more than to see the al Jawadis restored to their throne, when the cup of opportunity he had worked for all his life was within his grasp…this was the agenda that his grandfather had set him: not to embark on the great task that he had spent his life preparing for, not to begin the restoration of derelict family properties, not to start on the rehabilitation of the tragically mismanaged farms and land—but to court and marry a spoiled Westerner with no sense of duty.

The first time he set eyes on Princess Noor al Jawadi Durrani, Bari had realized that fate was laughing at him. His fears of what she might be were nothing compared to the reality of the beautiful, capricious woman he saw at the coronation. A magnificently spoiled woman with a sulky, sensual mouth, who had discovered that she was a princess in Bagestan and was taking the title to heart.

Her sexual magnetism had reached him even across

the expanse of the Great Hall of the Old Palace—him and a dozen other men. It sparked out from her, wild and undisciplined, like a new star in the heavens not sure of its own brilliance.

She smiled on all, and he saw men drawn to her without volition, like moths to the brightest light. Why will ten moths all be drawn to the only lantern in a caravanserai, when each could have the exclusive light of one of numerous lesser candles?

So it was with Noor.

In spite of his furious inner rejection of all his grandfather's interference, he could not help the jealous possessiveness that had invaded his spirit at that moment.

If she was to be his, then she would be all his.

For the first time in his life, Bari understood the instinct that had driven his forefathers to cloister and veil their women. He had not wanted her, did not choose her—but she was his. Those other men's eyes, caressing her, the smiles they received, he could hardly bear. They stole what was his—he felt the instinct of his blood rise up and tell him it was so.

He had found his reaction incomprehensible—some primitive instinct in his blood he had never before encountered engulfed him, and all for a woman he didn't know and half despised!

But wanted. Her dress was designed for maximum erotic impact—with glittering jewels clinging to her neck and breasts and clouds of green tulle cloaking and revealing her soft skin in tantalizing unpredictability.

If he had been worried about his ability to woo her, however, the worry was short-lived. She might be a Westerner in her contempt for arranged marriage, but love was no more on her agenda than on his. She was flattered by his interest, she preened herself in the intensity of his focus on her—but it hadn't taken him long to discover that she *felt* nothing.

He had attractions enough to win her. He was rich, his blood was noble, he was a Cup Companion and he socialized with the rich and famous from her world and his own.

Those were the traits she admired in him.

So he had showed her his family's wealth and position, instead of his hopes and dreams, as he might have done with a different woman. He had introduced her to celebrities and princes instead of his inner self. He had showered her with gifts instead of the undelivered kisses that burned him like live coals and acid.

For that was the worst torment of all—his desire for her. There was no rhyme or reason to it, and no reasoning, either, could change it.

He kept the other men away from her. She had not guarded her virginity all this time for him to lose the prize at the end. One look was usually enough, from Bari al Khalid. But if it was not—well, he knew how to enlighten a man's wilful ignorance.

He had known that she was sexually aware of him. Had known that she feared her own weakness, if he decided to press her. He had laid his plans as carefully as Prince Ashraf had in his bid for the throne of Bagestan. Noor had only one shield against him—the shield of *only-with-my-husband*. Well, then, he would remove that shield—he would build her to a pitch of desire, then propose and make love to her at once.

She would not say no to him sexually once he had stripped her of her shield, and equally she would not say no to marriage once he had deflowered her.

She would be caught in a trap she had made herself.

It had never once occurred to him that, having been

so neatly caught, she would execute an eleventh-hour escape. How could he have dreamed that, having accepted and agreed, their bargain sealed with lovemaking, she would change her mind and bolt?

At first he didn't know how to credit the reason she gave him for her flight. Why would she, who had shown no sign of love for him, no interest in his feelings, run when she learned that his grandfather had ordered him to marry her? Why should she balk at the thought of an arranged marriage, who had so ruthlessly "arranged" her own?

But now he saw the truth with chilling clarity. She had fled the wedding because she wanted everything, this woman who gave nothing, and she had learned at the last moment that she was not getting quite everything. How dared she assume that, in addition to everything else, she had his love—love she hadn't tried to return, hadn't even troubled to ask for, but nevertheless expected as her due?

It was not her due. No more than wealth and an easy life was universal admiration her due. *It behooves those to whom life has been generous to cultivate humility in the face of their good fortune.* He had learned that from an early age. It was the hallmark of a Cup Companion to offer service in exchange for such good fortune as noble birth and inherited wealth.

Noor stirred and sighed beside him, and he turned to watch her again. Under the foil sheet they shared she was wrapped in the white silk that she had cut from the skirts of her wedding dress. Above her head her wedding veil protected her from insects. He shook his head. Her wedding finery had made the same journey as his own hopes. They, too, had been abased.

Her eyelashes cast long shadows on her moon-whitened cheeks, giving her the fragile delicacy of a moon creature. The old romances talked of the jinn, a race of creatures made of fire, as humans were made of earth. Just now, with the pale glow playing over her flawless skin, it seemed as if the moonlight came from within. If Allah was moved to make creatures from earth and fire, Bari found himself thinking, then surely he must also have created some from moonlight. And such a being would look like this—her skin translucent, as though her light reflected on the heavens. As if the moon were her reflection.

Did the moon have a heart? Or was its pale light symbolic of cool heartlessness?

He had to marry her. Whatever her reasons for running from the wedding, he had to find the way back. That was the price of everything he had worked towards, all that he had dreamed for his family. That was the price of fulfilling his father's deathbed request—*go home, my son, and rebuild what we lost.*

He had given his father his word, at the impressionable age of fifteen, and the promise had thereafter consumed his life.

But there was another dream, too.

He wanted a partner in life. A woman to share its joys and sorrows with him. A woman capable of the giving and the sacrifice that marriage and family demanded. Not a woman of the careless selfishness Noor exhibited.

Once he had hoped that, in spite of everything, Noor had a heart and it was not out of his reach. That she would learn to love him, and he her. That whatever its beginnings, with time they could forge the kind of marriage that would be a strength to them both.

Her flight had awakened him from a blind and brazen foolishness. What if she had no heart to reach? Or what if he was not the one to touch it? Either way, there was misery in store, not just for him, but for any children they might have. For his mother and sisters, who would suffer, too.

Unless Noor had more heart than she had shown so far, one of his dreams he must give up. Either the dream of fulfilling his promise to his father and his duty to the family, or the dream of a good marriage. He knew he could have only one. He must betray either his heritage, or his own heart. He had to choose.

Bari looked out at the jewel-spangled darkness that surrounded them. Noble birth and wealth and beauty were useless commodities here on this deserted island. Only the real inner qualities of the person mattered now…and here, too, would they not be revealed?

His eyes narrowed, staring out, as if the future might lie concealed in the blackness of the night. *The true heart is revealed in adversity.* It was a proverb in his family, which had been recited many times during the decades of suffering when Ghasib remained in power.

Noor was dreaming. He watched a frown chase across her brow, then the whisper of a smile drawing at one cheek. Unexpectedly his heart kicked, and his body leaped with hunger. If he reached for her now, if he drew her into the hungry embrace of his body and arms, if she awoke to his kiss and his desire—could she reject him?

He knew she couldn't. Even without the drug of sleep invading her mind and limbs, even without the magic of the stars overhead, the silence, the scents of nature on the breeze—she would be his. The fire in his blood would heat hers.

She was a naturally passionate woman. He had learned that during their one heady afternoon and evening of delight. Whatever lies she had held in her heart, her body had told another truth.

His flesh pulsed painfully, wanting her. Wanting that soft breathing to change, as it had before, into hungry moans of desire and delight. Wanting the taste, the smell, the touch of her, the inner flame and welcoming moistness that had almost sent him over the edge with the first thrust of possession.

The smell and the sound of the sea was a piercing reminder of that afternoon he had stolen from reality. Involuntarily he lowered his face towards the curve of her throat. The scent of her skin after their hard labour was pungent with musk and, remembering, his body tightened convulsively.

She should have been his. This was by rights his wedding night! If she had not been such a little fool, he would now have every right to awaken her with the kisses that burned his mouth, to stroke the firm, soft swell of her breasts that only the moonlight now caressed, to feed the growing hunger of her blood with his mouth, his tongue, his hands, and finally his body.

He would have the right to push his hardened flesh into the soft depths of her—his wife, his other self. To thrust and thrust in a repeat of that wild seeking—the wildest he had ever known, to feel her answer in her flesh as surely as he heard it in her throat.

Bari lifted his head with an effort and gazed out over the moon-kissed sea.

He was nearly certain that the island they were on was the most remote of the Gulf Islands, a straggler at the very tip of the chain, called Solomon's Foot. If so, it was well out of the way of any major shipping lanes. And all small-boat traffic among the islands had ended with the evacuations. The only vessels visiting the is-

lands now were the dhows and ferries that supplied the
Gulf Eden Resort. Their route would bring them nowhere near this island.

If the proverb were true—if the truth of her would
be revealed in adversity—what better opportunity for it
could he ask than this? To be alone with her, in a place
where they would be utterly dependent on themselves
and each other. For everything. Food, shelter, compan-
ionship, security…pleasure.

And if she did have a heart, what better opportunity
could he hope to find for learning whether it could ever
be his? There was another saying among the men in his
family: *a man opens a woman's heart by repeated
knocking at the door of the womb.* It was a reminder that
sexual prowess is any lover's most powerful asset.

The moon climbed higher in the sky, white and pure
and unshockable, as Bari made his plans.

Nine

Noor awoke as those who live in the natural world have done since humankind's beginning—with the rising of the sun. It came up out of the sea like a knot of molten gold serpents, flaming and twisting against the blushing sky.

Bari was standing looking out over the water.

"Awake?" he murmured as she stirred and lay watching the spectacular unfoldment of the first scene in the drama of the day. Birdsong rippled over them from the forest.

Noor yawned and leaned up on one elbow. "Who could sleep through this!" She dragged the makeshift mosquito net down and moved to sit up, then winced and moved more carefully. Every muscle seemed to have taken a beating.

"Oooh," she groaned weakly. "I think I need a chiropractor. Everything feels out of place."

Bari watched as she lifted one arm to admire an

angry bruise. "There will be something for that in the first aid kit."

Noor nodded and got to her feet. "At least it won't be permanently disfiguring."

She stretched gingerly. In spite of everything it was invigorating to spend a night in the open when the air was so fresh. She tried an experimental bit of jogging on the spot. Nothing hurt too, too much. She'd actually felt worse after days when her personal trainer had been in a mean mood.

"I don't know how I'm going to manage my work-out," she murmured thoughtfully. Without her gym equipment, how would she get the kinks out?

Suddenly she noticed the expression on Bari's face. "What's your problem?" she challenged him.

He shook his head, laughing. "Not a word, Princess. Would you like a drink?"

In instant answer, Noor's stomach growled, and she discovered she was ravenous.

"My God, so this is hunger!"

Bari collected the water jug from the raft and measured out a small amount for her in the plastic cup.

She swirled the rainwater around on her tongue. How weird it tasted! As if no taste at all could result in a bad taste. She looked into Bari's amused eyes and decided not to share that little experience with him.

"I'm starved. Let's eat!"

"It will be best to forage before the day gets hot," he agreed. "Afterwards we must—"

"Forage?" she repeated blankly. "What are you talking about?"

His eyes opened with a look that made her want to hit him. "About going to hunt for something to eat. Isn't that what you said?"

Noor laughed in merry disbelief. "Oh, sure! A little stroll down to Cocoa's for some skinny latte and a fat-free muffin!"

"We won't know how difficult it is until we try." He took an equal measure of water himself and tossed it off in one mouthful, then glanced up at the sun now making a fiery ascent up the cobalt-blue sky. "We should start now. It will get hot quickly."

"You have to be joking! What am I supposed to do— pick berries into a palm leaf?"

"Unless you have more aggressive survival skills."

"Is *that* what you call it!"

Bari looked at her in frowning, silent consideration for a moment. Then he half smiled.

"Noor, this is not a joke. How are you proposing to eat until rescue arrives?"

"We've got rations. I saw them." She knew he knew they were there, so what was his game?

He stood in front of her in an easy pose, his feet firmly at home in the soft grey-white sand, his arms crossed over his chest, the little plastic glass dangling from one finger. His silk jacket was creased and stained, and so were the white trousers, but he still had the proud, unmistakable bearing of a Cup Companion.

It had always thrilled her before. Now it seemed to be turned against her, and she found the condescending reproof of his nod seriously irritating.

"Yes, a very few rations were in the plane's grab bag. We must save them for emergencies, however. I am sorry, but with a little luck—"

"This feels like an emergency to me," Noor interrupted stiffly. "I'm starved!"

"Nothing like appetite for sharpening the hunter-gatherer instinct," Bari said, in the manner of a tolerant drill sergeant with a lazy new recruit. He turned and put the water back into the life raft, and closed the Velcro fastenings. Then he turned. "Come."

"I don't have any shoes, or have you forgotten? Or clothes."

He looked down at his own bare feet, and then at her, with an expression on his face that irritated her royally, and took her wrist in a strong, careless, but unmistakably autocratic hold.

"Your feet will soon toughen up."

"I don't want my feet to 'toughen up'!" She was sure that he was playing a game. She dug her heels into the sand, pulling her hand from the firm clasp of his own. "And I'm not going hunting barefoot and in my underwear!"

A sudden peal of birdsong underlined the silence.

Bari rested an assessing gaze on her. "What, then? Do you prefer to go hungry?"

"Can't you bring me back something?" she demanded. "You're the big, strong primitive male, after all! You're the one with the ceremonial sword!"

Some change in him made her shift uncomfortably. But really, it was ridiculous! What was she supposed to do half-naked, shoeless and weaponless, in a forest?

"By tradition, yes, I should be your protector," he said. "But yesterday you rejected tradition, and you rejected me. I am nothing to you now, and you—" his eyes narrowed "—you are nothing to me, Noor. You can't run from me one day and demand my protection the next. If you want breakfast, you will have to help find it."

She knew she was on dangerous ground, but unaccustomed hunger was making her mulish. "I have found it! It's in those neat little plastic packs of emergency rations over there in the raft! And that's all the hunting-gathering I'm going to do this morning, thanks!"

She stepped forward, but his hand on her shoulder, very firm now, stopped her.

"I think we have already established that in a battle between brains and brawn, brawn inevitably wins. Do you care to put it to the test one more time?"

She looked at him and saw nothing but implacable determination. His eyes were the colour of volcanic lava—the surface black, but with lines of glowing light hinting at a fierce, banked heat within. Was it her imagination, or was that red-gold line of fracture a little wider now?

She used to imagine that what she saw was a deep dynamo of passion—but he had been faking that. What was the source, then, of that half compelling, half dangerous heat?

She was convinced that the man who had yesterday been prepared to marry her would now watch her starve without a flicker of conscience. Noor could just imagine him taking pleasure from eating his bloody kill in front of her without offering her a morsel. Yet the Bari she had known until yesterday—thought she had known—would have acted very differently in these circumstances.

That curious sense of two time streams brushed her again. Suppose she had married Bari, and suppose they had taken off for their honeymoon and been brought down by the storm, ending up here, exactly where they were. How would he be treating her now?

She laughed aloud. "You know, all things considered, I'm pretty lucky! It's not very nice learning that a man's a monster, but it could be a lot worse, couldn't it? I could be discovering right now that I was *married* to a monster!"

"A man protects his wife," he contradicted her in a gravelly voice. "You are not my wife, by your own choice. Why does that make me a monster?"

Something like regret reached for her, but she shook herself out of its stealthy grip, bent to toss aside the gold foil sheet, picked up the rectangle of white silk she had slept on last night, and wrapped it around herself. It didn't offer much more actual protection than the skimpy teddy underneath, but psychologically, just here and just now, it was almost as good as putting on armour.

She pulled the knot of her makeshift sarong tight above her breast, staring at him as she did so.

With an arrogant blink that was his excuse for a nod, Bari turned and went over to the beached raft again, bending to search inside. When he straightened, he was tucking the knife into his waistband.

"Not packing the ancestral sword today?" Noor commented brightly.

"It is a battle sword," Bari told her softly. "It would be sullied by the blood of the hunt." She wasn't sure if he was joking, or speaking for effect, or telling the simple truth.

"Common sense somehow suggests," she remarked sweetly, "that a hunter has to get a lot closer to his prey with a knife than with a three-foot blade, but I'm not going to argue with the great warrior!"

"It would be a waste of time, and you are hungry," he agreed pleasantly. Noor stifled her reaction to that, except for the flashing glance that bounced right off him.

He led her along the beach towards the rocks and the higher ground at the southern tip. He wanted to measure out the island, get more of an idea of where they were, before he risked a trek in among the trees.

It was a beautiful walk along the increasingly rocky beach in the morning sunlight, with birdsong coming from a forest that was much more extensive than it had appeared—a giant oasis.

Noor resolutely refused to voice her surprise. But Bari answered the unspoken question.

"The islands, like the coastal regions of the Barakat Emirates and, to a lesser extent, Bagestan, are very fertile," he explained. "Even after thirty years of Ghasib's mismanagement. Several herbs that grow only here are known for their healing properties and used to be exported to the mainland by the islanders."

Reluctant laughter burst from her. "I thought that was just my parents' fantasy of the old country! They always said it was the Garden of Eden."

"There is good rainfall here, probably the same climate that covered a much larger area in antiquity. Some geophysical archaeologists suggest that a huge area—from the Mediterranean to the mountains of Parvan—once was as lush as this tiny area of the gulf. But catastrophic climate change affected the rainfall and, bit by bit, turned the once-fertile land into desert."

She was tacitly agreeing to a truce, perhaps because the nature of their expedition made them both feel they should be united. Exploring an unknown world, however benign it might prove, made comrades of them.

"No one knows why this tiny area escaped the march of the desert. The prolonged drought in Bagestan has raised fears that the process of desertification may even be starting again. But for the moment, we live in the last corner of the paradise that Adam and Eve knew."

Paradise. Alone in paradise with Bari al Khalid.

I don't think so! Noor told herself dryly.

The black rock, when they began to climb, wasn't as hard on her bare feet as Noor had feared. It was smoother than she had guessed from a distance, a little glassy, as if, perhaps, from a long-distant volcanic eruption. And she supposed it was exercise of a sort, if not as regimented as her workout.

"This rock is mysterious in origin," Bari continued in tour-guide mode. "It exists in the Gulf of Barakat and nowhere else on the planet. Experts argue as to its origins. There is little agreement."

They found a trail, narrow but freshly used, as they climbed higher.

"Do you think there's someone living here after all?" Noor asked, a little breathless with exertion and hope.

Bari shrugged.

"If so, they have arrived only recently. After Ghasib leased the development rights for all the islands to the Gulf Eden Resort chain a couple of years ago, the inhabitants of the islands were forcefully evacuated, and their homes and villages destroyed. The developers planned to create an isolated luxury resort for tourists."

"It was a big story at home," Noor remembered. "People were so outraged."

"Yes, an international outcry delayed the development, and now the Sultan is under pressure to turn the islands into a wildlife sanctuary. But the evacuees have to be considered. Many had lived on the islands for generations. Since the Return, some have been trying to re-establish their homes on the islands."

Noor looked hopefully around for signs of human occupation. People meant boats. Boats meant getting away from her ex-husband-to-be and his insistence on a return to stone-age living.

Bari knelt to examine some spoor. "Sorry," he told her dryly, as if her face had been too revealing. "This path has been created by animals. Goats, possibly."

"Not my lucky day, then," said Noor sharply.

They couldn't climb very high—the slope was too

steep. When they had got as high as they could, accompanied by the screech of seagulls wheeling and banking around the stony peak, they stopped to get their bearings.

The island, a small, somewhat squashed oval, was lying roughly northeast-southwest. It was generally flat, except at the southern tip, where it pushed upward into a peak of rugged black rock.

It was a breathtaking sight. At their backs the peak seemed slightly concave, a petrified wave arcing over them. They stood in the lee, just where the vegetation lost its hold. Below they could see the goat track they had been following trace the curve of the hillside and then lead down to the forested slope below.

White sand beach curved around more than half of the oval. The southern third, under the peak, was black rock. On the opposite side to the beach where they had landed was a reedy area which Bari said was a mudflat. Within the protection of the rocky peak nestled a green paradise of trees, birds and flowers. The sound of water told them there must be a stream nearby, and down below, a regular break in the rich greenery indicated its path.

A brightly coloured bird shrieked and flapped up towards the sun before tucking its wings and diving back down in among the trees.

Bari suddenly pointed to a spot at about their eye level. After a moment she saw it, a large bird, its wings outspread, riding the currents.

"A falcon," he said in satisfaction.

"Why is that good?"

"It means there are small animals."

But however they strained, in whatever direction, there was no sign of land.

After a few minutes they followed the track along the

lightly treed slope, with the sound of running water getting closer and closer.

Suddenly there it was in front of them: a small, delicate waterfall like a bridal veil tumbling down to where it was captured in a sparkling stream a few feet below them in the black rock. From there the water ran in a series of streams and tiny falls down to the forest floor below.

A small black-and-white goat stood precariously on the rocks, drinking from the water swirling in the bowl-shaped cavity of a rock.

It had not noticed their approach. Bari and Noor stood watching, silenced by the little animal's vulnerability. It was so totally trusting, eyes closed, nose deep in the life-giving stream, the perfect embodiment of that state of grace which allows the Arabic language to assign "peace" and "submission" the same word.

Noor glanced at Bari and exchanged a rueful smile. By wordless agreement, the two humans sank silently to the ground and waited for the goat to finish its drink. The animal's complete trust was somehow compelling—beautiful and deeply touching.

"How easy it is to love creatures who trust," Noor thought, and was a little surprised to find that she had whispered the words.

Bari's gaze rested on her thoughtfully, but he did not reply.

The goat lifted its head and gazed at them for a moment before turning to spring up the few feet to the path. Then, as they watched in silence, it wandered unafraid among the trees and began to forage.

Noor glanced down at the knife tucked into Bari's waistband, then up into his face. He laughed as if reading her thoughts.

"I'd have to be a lot hungrier," he agreed.

Noor laughed with him, and for a moment it was the way it used to be between them, and she remembered with sharp nostalgia how she had imagined that they were well suited. That their sense of humour matched.

But all the time they had been laughing at different things. Bari had been laughing at her.

Her gaze returned to the delicious little waterfall. After a moment's pause they simultaneously began to strip off and, leaving their clothes, clambered down the rocks to stand under the lacy tumble of water.

It was cold enough to seem icy on their exercise-heated bodies, and Noor involuntarily gasped as the fat drops pelted her.

His ears heard, and his body remembered, that it was the same gasp she had given the first time he entered her. The flesh of her breasts tightened, too, in a way he remembered in that very different moment. Bari stood under a strong, steady fall of cool water, his back to her.

"What a relief to get the salt and sand off my skin!" Noor cried.

Nervousness pitched her voice high and thin, but she hoped Bari wouldn't notice. She had to struggle not to devour him with her eyes. They had made love only on that one long, never-to-be-forgotten afternoon, and one afternoon, she discovered, wasn't long enough to create an immunity to the sight of him naked.

His body was like an aftershave ad, water droplets passionately clinging to perfect proportions. It was hard to keep her eyes from drinking him in in the same way they had everything else this incredible morning—with gratitude for the beauty.

Bari barely glanced at her. "It's good luck that we have a source of fresh water." His voice was as distant as his eyes.

After a minute Noor reached for the teddy that she had left on a rock, and began busily scrubbing it between her knuckles as she stood under the flow.

Bari put his head under, then emerged spluttering and shaking his head. Vital animal grace emanated from him so powerfully she felt it like a physical touch. Water streamed down his face and body, tracing every curvature of muscle and bone with loving attention, as though nature herself were memorizing his shape in order to produce so fine a work again elsewhere.

Noor's womb clenched with the primitive, unconscious understanding that her own body might serve as nature's workshop for such a project. What hit her then was a bolt of electricity that seemed to come not from the sky, but from the rocks under her feet, inescapably shooting up through her body to her scalp.

There was a moment of stillness all around them then, during which the lacy waterfall seemed to capture the sunlight and multiply it into a thousand diamonds tossed and tumbling over the rocks onto their heads.

In that moment, strong and strange, a man and a woman gazed at each other, and through each other into a world of possibility. The soft wind whispered to them that their two selves held the key to the great secret. The man put out his hand, and the woman's hand would have been unerringly drawn to its embrace, even had she been blind.

Their bodies sparkling with diamonds and gold, he led her to a soft sun-kissed place, and drew her down to lie with him.

Ten

$\mathbf{A}$ shock of heat embraced her as she lay on him, her legs entangling with his as naturally as if they had met this way over a thousand lifetimes past. Her body, resting against his aroused flesh, melted with anticipation, and in answer his hand gripped the firm mound of her behind and held her ruthlessly as his hips rose of their own accord to lift against her.

His fingers slipped around her thighs and began to tease and stroke the delicate folds of the flower, and his eyes watched her face, devouring every sign of her desire for him.

She was so moist, inviting the long, strong fingers to slip inside that almost-virgin space and warn her body of the delights to come.

Meanwhile the fingers of his other hand cupped her head, weaving through the damp tangles of her hair and drawing her face down to his waiting mouth. The hungry kisses that he had been holding back for too long burned up to scorch his lips as his mouth took possession of hers.

"Bari," she murmured, half protesting, but he smothered the sound with his kiss.

Noor felt the touch of those knowing, tender fingers ignite a hot sweetness that melted all through her, and her legs spread with pulsing hunger, falling wide to give him access to the deepest part of herself as honeyed urgency tightened her skin.

His fingers vibrated in her, his tongue following suit in the moist depths of her mouth, until she tore her lips from his with a cry, lifting away to arch her back into the pleasure building in her. His other hand moved down then, pressing her, moulding her lower body against his hardened flesh, until, with soft panting cries, she welcomed the flooding heat that coursed through her.

Her face to the smiling sky, she groaned out her gratitude, but the hypnotic motion of his hands paused only a moment, and then began anew.

"Again," he commanded.

This time the explosion came more quickly, and then leaped to another buildup, and another, while Noor writhed with increasing openness, her cries of completion and excitement grew louder, the pleasure more intense…and her desire for more grew greedier.

Her throat was wide open, her head back, her body arched, her thighs clenching, her hunger deep and animal. She was just where he wanted her—in that land where she recognized only sensation. Heat was here, and rippling pleasure, and shivering joy, and delicious moistness—but she knew no more than that.

He watched with his hunger written on his face, a hunger he could not disguise. Her head was back, her eyes squeezed shut, all her being focused on pleasure like nothing she had known existed.

Finally he could wait no longer. His control whipped from his grasp like a cable that breaks under too much weight, and his hands lifted her, opening her for him, and his body leaped in one fierce thrust. And with that sudden, hard urgency, there was what she had been seeking, what her hunger had waited for: the fierce plea-sure-pain of his body ruthless in hers, and the soaring desire that swooped and wheeled with the motion of the falcon above.

He pulled her knees down beside his hips, fixed his strong hands around her waist, and taught her the mo-tions of that primitive dance: down and up and down and up, over and over, wild and free, until the god answered, and pleasure rained down on them.

As soon as the last heaves of satisfaction had died in her, Noor started kicking herself inwardly. What kind of fool for punishment was she? Bari al Khalid had cyn-ically taken her virginity when he didn't love her, had tricked her—what kind of stupid, masochistic weak-ness was it to let him get to her all over again? She lifted his arm from her and sat up.

"I suppose you think that proved something," she said.

Only with my husband, she had always promised herself. And since she wouldn't marry Bari now to save her life, she shouldn't have made love with him again. She turned and looked down at him.

His head was turned towards her, the black eyes half-lidded. He said nothing.

What really made her bitter was the little voice that said that since she was no longer a virgin it didn't re-ally matter anymore, and the pleasure was worth it. That was exactly the attitude that she had despised in her friends. *Who do I hurt? It's not a diminishing commodity. We only get one life.*

She had thought she was safe from all that. But it seemed sex was like a drug. Once you got a taste of it—

Her anger suddenly shifted its target. How dared he make love to her, after what he had said about her? And why?

Noor got to her feet and tied the sarong over her breasts.

"Just more cynical manipulation," she accused as she picked up the wet teddy and wrung it out with an angry twist.

"Why would I want to manipulate you?" His voice was expressive of nothing so much as boredom, and her outrage flared.

"Your grandfather's estates *are* still an issue, I suppose!" Noor responded sharply.

"Oh, that."

She smiled, showing her teeth.

"My grandfather will have the good sense to realize that however good the tree, some fruit is always spoiled. When he learns of it he will not wish me to marry a woman who has acted the way you did."

Noor flinched but stood her ground. "So it was just a freebie, then?" she mocked. "Just the typical male grab-it-while-you-can?"

"And what was it from the typical female point of view? Rape, I suppose?"

She was too angry to answer.

Under the white *shalwar* he had been wearing a snug thong, and it seemed that was all he meant to put on now. He slung his wet shirt and trousers over one shoulder.

"Very Tarzan," Noor said, mock-admiringly. "I advise you not to mistake me for Jane again, if you don't want a very uncomfortable surprise."

"Who the hell is Tarzan?" Bari asked, as if it was the last thing he cared to know.

They breakfasted on fresh herbs, raw dates and baked turtle's eggs eaten off palm leaves. Not exactly a meal for the gods, but she was hungry enough to swallow every morsel. She could have eaten more, but Bari had insisted on taking only a few eggs out of the nest they found.

"But there are hundreds of eggs there!" Noor had protested.

"And there is a reason for that. We are not the turtle's only predators. And they are a rare species."

She couldn't argue with that, but a couple of eggs didn't make much of a meal when there was no bread or salad or anything else to accompany them.

Licking her fingers, she looked around. "Well, what now?" she wondered aloud. "Think we'll see a boat soon?"

"The first necessity is to build a shelter."

She looked at him, suspecting a trick. "What's wrong with the raft?"

"It's too small, and it gets too hot. Over the long term, psychologically, we need—"

"But we're bound to be rescued!"

"Possibly, but what if we are not? Do you expect the world to rush to save your life when you will do nothing to save yourself?"

"You're just trying to scare me. You want to punish me for running away and you think hard work will do the trick!"

It was close enough to the truth to wring a dry smile out of him. He crossed well-muscled arms over his naked chest and eyed her levelly.

"I think it won't hurt you to put some effort into your own continued existence," he agreed.

"I've already had the hunter-gatherer lecture this morning, thanks. I think that's enough for one day. Build your own damn shelter!"

He regarded her in silence for a long uncomfortable moment. Noor put her chin up.

"This is not television, Noor. There is no camera, no crew. We don't get airlifted out if we get stomach cramp. This is real life."

She lifted her eyebrows expressively. "So?"

"Cooperation is the first rule of survival."

"Really! I'm sure there's a second rule."

He wasn't rising to the bait. He said, as if she had asked in good faith, "The second is, elect one person as leader, and then obey his commands."

"Let me guess. You've been elected."

A little voice in her suggested how unwise it was to embark on such a futile battle. *No stupider than his insistence on building a shelter,* Noor dismissed it.

Bari smiled, showing strong white teeth in the smile that she used to think was handsome. Now it just made him look like a wild animal.

"Brawn gets fifty-one percent of the vote, I think we agreed."

"Well, brawn can just go ahead and build one hundred percent of the shelter! Brains is going to do the logical thing and use the life raft when necessary."

"Wrong again. We'll take the canopy to waterproof the roof of the shelter."

"Oh, brilliant! Cut up our shelter in order to make a shelter!" she mocked admiringly. "Well, at least you're not claiming the monopoly on brains!"

"Can you possibly be imagining that your continued

mulishness is a sign of intelligence? You are acting like a fool! What do you know of conditions here? We may be completely out of the shipping lane on this island. It might be days, weeks, bef—"

"I don't believe for a minute it will be weeks, and I happen to think the raft is a good enough temporary shelter."

"No. What you think about a shelter is nothing to do with this. You are resisting what I say because you feel cheated. You blame me for not being in love with you."

"Wrong!" Noor carolled hotly. "Since we are no longer going to get married, I couldn't care less what you think of me."

"But this is not the time for such resistance," he went on, as if she hadn't spoken. "We must act to survive. You know this. Even if only psychologically, shelter is of crucial importance to us both. Now, I will give orders and I expect to be obeyed."

"You seem to think you've got me at your mercy. Suppose I disappoint your expectations?"

"Then I will leave you here and go and establish my camp elsewhere. You will not be welcome there."

She knew he wouldn't. He couldn't! But his black eyes held an expression she didn't trust. As if he *wanted* her to give him the excuse to abandon her.

"I must have been totally deluded to imagine you loved me!" she said bitterly, capitulating.

"But self-delusion is almost a way of life with you," Bari replied softly.

The next few days were sheer, unrelieved hell. Bari was a slave driver. On a diet of baked turtles' eggs, raw dates, and some berries that hardly deserved the name, he expected her to hew trees, haul branches, salvage the blackened remains of a tragic little village, and act as general dogsbody in his grandiose building scheme.

Her nails became unbelievably grimed and filthy, her legs and arms scratched and bruised and streaked with black that wouldn't wash off, the skin of her face so dry and sunburned she was sure it would never recover its tone, her nose peeling, her hair matted so she couldn't even get her fingers through it. And as for her palms and soles—how could blisters get blisters?

She looked like a total bag lady, and she knew it. The orange "moccasins" she had been forced to make for herself, cutting pieces from the leftover bits of the rubber-and-canvas canopy of the raft and painstakingly stitching them together with the fishing line, were ugly and uncomfortable. Also scant protection from snakes, the thought of which terrified her. On her head and over her fading and greying teddy, she wore a succession of soiled, stained scarves and sarongs that offered her insufficient protection from the sun, especially on a breezy day, got filthy the moment she put a fresh one on, and mostly got in her way when she was doing the menial, degrading work that Bari constantly assigned her as her share of their survival task. Her hips and abdomen and breasts were now tanned with the pattern of the lace on her teddy, which she scrubbed and put on again every day.

Bari, naturally, had a change of clothes. The emergency grab bag from the plane had contained not only a lighter, an all-purpose Leatherman tool, and a large spool of plastic tape, all of which were proving seriously useful, but also a pair of denim shorts.

That was all, just shorts. But there were days when Noor would have paid any price for the luxury of a zipper closing.

Worst was the lack of anything approaching civilized toilet facilities, even paper, and although Bari had promised to build something when the shelter was closer to complete, it seemed a long time coming.

It was the first time in her adult life that Noor had spent even twenty-four hours without liberal applications of soap, shampoo, deodorant and perfume, never mind toilet tissue.

The only relief she had from this life of horrors was a toothbrush and miniature tube of toothpaste, also from the grab bag. Since there was only one, they shared it, and the toothpaste was severely rationed, but the daily taste of civilization was all that stood between Noor and an irredeemably primitive existence. Some days she almost wept from sheer gratitude as she brushed her teeth.

They rested in the hottest part of the afternoon, because not even Bari could force anyone to work in such crippling heat. But even so, Noor didn't rest. Every day, no matter how exhausted she was, she made the trek up the mountain—and it seemed more and more like a real mountain with each trip—to take a freshwater shower in the magical little waterfall. It always soothed her to be in such a peaceful place. But it was impossible to get really clean, and by the time she had returned to the campsite she was pouring with sweat again.

In the catalogue of woes of this castaway existence, Noor found that the worst came at night. Not only was sleeping on the sand uncomfortable, not only was she often too cold to sleep, but when she did sleep she would be startled awake by the strange noises. After what had happened at the waterfall, they slept apart. Nights, she learned, were cool, and Noor had nothing to put on except the thin teddy and her homemade sarongs.

No matter how snugly she wrapped herself in a foil sheet, when a breeze blew, as happened nearly every night, it succeeded in lifting the sheet. All her built-up body heat could disappear in a second.

Chivalry dictated that Bari should offer her his jacket at night, but Bari, it seemed, wasn't going to be dictated to by any code of gentlemanly conduct. He wore the jacket on his head during the day, and as a shirt at night, and Noor was left to make do with her bits of silk. She had tried wearing the bodice of the wedding dress, but it wasn't practicable—the sleeves were awkwardly tight when she turned it back to front, and it was covered with pearls, and there were no buttons.

"I've already told you—you rejected my protection. On what grounds do you make a claim for it now?" he said when she raised the subject one evening, after a particularly gruelling day, as the sun went down and she faced another sleepless night.

"Do I have to explain ordinary civilized behaviour to you?" Noor cried.

Bari laughed with biting mockery. "Yes, let me hear Princess Noor's explanation of ordinary civilized behaviour!"

She wanted to tell him where he could put it, but the trouble was, she needed him and his masculine protection, however little she wanted it.

"You're bigger and stronger, and men have more reserves of body heat, or something," she said. "You've also got the warmest piece of clothing. Doesn't that equation suggest to you that you should share?"

When she saw the expression on his face, she knew she'd let herself in for something, but it was too late to recall the words.

"And you, Noor—you are beautiful, and graceful, and extremely charming when you want to be. And yet—how much generosity of spirit did you show to my mother and sisters? Did you share that charm with them?"

"Oh, will you leave it *alone!*" Noor exclaimed impatiently, jumping up to stride around the fire that was cooking today's fish.

"All right! I acted like a spoiled brat, I admit it, all right?" She flung out her hands. "I was wrong and selfish…and pretty damned stupid, if you want the truth. So stupid that I didn't even realize I was making them dislike me! Does my confession satisfy you? I'm *sorry,* but now I'm stuck on this island, and I can't do anything to make amends to your mother till we get back to civilization! I promise you, I'll abase myself to everyone I've insulted as soon as we get out of this hole! In the meantime, I'm freezing to death at night and not getting any sleep, and I have no stamina to get through what you'll admit is a pretty hellish existence, with you constantly badgering me and making me do the dirty work!"

"All the work is dirty work," Bari said flatly.

"All right, yes! You're working just as hard—harder! I agree. But I am not used to it, and you're not exactly making it easy for me, are you?"

"How would you like me to make it easy for you?" he asked with silky calm. "By doing everything myself?"

She could hardly keep the lid on. "No!" she shouted. "*Not* by doing it all yourself, though I know that's no more than your opinion of me! But would it hurt you to empathize a little?"

She was striding up and down, flinging her arms around for punctuation. "If it's my job to clean the fish, or gather wood, or hold a rope while you put up a wall, do you think you might say so courteously? Does it always have to come out of your mouth with contempt, as if you're utterly convinced that I resent lifting a finger to look after myself?"

"And don't you?"

For a moment the quiet question flummoxed her. She stopped and gazed at him across the fire.

"You act as if you resent lifting a finger to look after yourself, Noor. You seem to blame me for the deprivations you suffer, but who caused us to be in this situation? And as for the necessity to work, it is survival itself that makes these demands on you, not me."

Would he always succeed in putting her in the wrong? "I—I know that!" she faltered.

"If you really know it, then why do you not take on the responsibility for your existence as an adult, instead of responding to every demand like a spoiled child who prefers to play?"

"Do I do that?"

He was silent, leaving it to her own conscience to answer. Noor heaved a breath, trying to calm her jangled feelings.

"Do you think your constant bewailing of our position makes it easier for you, or for me?" he continued after a moment. "Why do you not accept the situation, Noor, instead of always regretting it? We are here together, and we need each other. You seem to want me to remember that fact, while you ignore it. But it takes two, Noor. Just like marriage."

Tears sprang to her eyes suddenly, but the sudden snapping of her overstretched emotions had nothing to do with that word *marriage*. She didn't regret not marrying Bari in the least, however much she might wish she'd found a better way to avoid it.

It was fatigue and stress and hunger that were the cause of her losing it like this. That and Bari's constant determination to hold up a mirror to her least attractive traits, and make sure she looked closely at them!

"I wish I could make *you* see yourself," she said, as tears spilled down her cheeks in spite of her fierce efforts to contain them. "You're not perfect, either, you know!"

"No," he agreed. "I'm not perfect, either. So what do you want from me, Noor?"

She sniffed. "I can't sleep because I get chilled. That's all."

"All right, I can warm you at night. Is that what you want?"

His rough, dark voice sent chills of a completely different kind through her. Whatever her conscious decision, she couldn't seem to get her body to agree that Bari's touch was poison to her.

Her eyes widened. What was he offering? "I—" She licked her lips. "What, you mean…"

He let the half words hang painfully in the silence, while the fire crackled merrily. His eyelids drooped, and he reached out and used a stick to prod the fish cooking on a palm leaf. Then he turned and gazed at her.

"Do you want sex?" he asked baldly. His voice was heavy with reluctance, and Noor cringed inwardly. If his tone expressed any approximation of his feelings…

"No!" she said, half-panicked at the thought that he should imagine she was angling for his lovemaking. "I told you!"

"So you did," he agreed in a bored voice. He nodded. "Although we are not the best examples of the fact, the most efficient warmth is human warmth," he said with ironic humour. "I will give you the jacket to wear in bed, since you ask so nicely, and I will share your bed for warmth only. Is that what you want?"

She felt unbelievably humiliated, without knowing

why. "Yes, please," she whispered. Then she had a thought. "Bari—"

"Noor?"

"I could…if you liked, I could make you a djellaba from my—my dress. I could braid some strips into a rope, too. Wouldn't that be easier than your jacket?"

His eyes blazed with an expression she hardly dared to read as approval. "Yes, it would be much easier. Thank you, Noor," he said gravely, and her heart swelled.

"I don't know why I didn't think of it days ago!" she exclaimed.

Bari smiled. "Don't you?" he asked.

Eleven

"Please let me find some soap," Noor begged as she gingerly lifted another blackened mud brick and tossed it onto the growing pile she was collecting.

They had found the site of the destroyed village on the second afternoon, and had immediately begun the dirtiest salvage operation she ever hoped to undertake. And here she was yet again, under the watchful eye of the little black-and-white goat, who had taken to following her whenever she was in the forest, but still was nervous about visiting the campsite.

Something had shifted for Noor. Although the work was still tedious, she experienced a sense of purpose. To be working to provide for her own needs gave her an odd kind of satisfaction—what she did, every minute of every day, was useful, necessary work. Bari was right. Without cooperation they would not survive, and there was pleasure in knowing that he needed her as much as she needed him, and that her work contributed to a larger, common goal.

Even the little goat seemed to need her, and she guessed that he had been a family pet and was lonely for human company. She was slowly teaching him that she could be trusted, and that there was nothing to fear at the campsite. And every day he trusted her a little more, and that was a surprisingly powerful source of comfort.

Still, she was almost constantly hungry. And their diet was unbelievably boring.

"The food is terrible—*and* there's not enough of it!" she joked to the goat now. The little animal gazed at her, chewing contentedly on a bright green leaf—one of the special herbs that Bari had pointed out to her, she saw.

"Oh, yeah, *you're* all right, Jack!" Noor said dryly.

They had found another turtle's nest, and every day they took a few eggs from one or the other, and carefully covered up the rest. They alternated between fish, the small animals Bari sometimes also caught, and eggs, and the root vegetables they sometimes found digging in the overgrown, deserted gardens in the village. Sometimes herbs lent a welcome piquancy to the food.

Noor had been driven almost crazy by the lack of salt until Bari pointed out that the sea was full of it. After several frustrating attempts, she had at last been rewarded by the sight of a few white crystals on her palm leaf. The taste had brought tears of relief to her eyes.

Her emotions were much too volatile, of course.

The growing torment now was the lack of soap. Her hair got more matted every day. A couple of times she had tried to see herself in a section of the foil sheet, but she was almost grateful that it was too wrinkled to reflect her image. Really, she had only to look at Bari to get a fair approximation of her own state. Bari's facial hair had progressed from shadow to stubble to bristles, and was now on the way to becoming a genuine beard.

He looked wild and uncivilized, his skin getting darker every day, his face dry and cracked, as hers must be. His strong, expressive hands were as grimed and callused as any construction worker's.

At least, thank God, however badly they needed soap, they couldn't really smell each other. Or at least, what she could smell of him was only pleasantly, if sharply, masculine.

She fervently hoped she returned the favour. Right now Noor would have traded her entire newly inherited fortune for one day—one hour!—in her favourite health club.

"Full-body Shiatsu Massage with Cucumber and Nine Essential Oils," she called lyrically to the little goat, straightening for a moment to ease her aching back. It was astonishing how little a regular workout seemed to have prepared her body for real work.

The goat stopped chewing and gazed at her with wide, half-fascinated eyes. "Manicure with Peach Essence Nail Rejuvenation Cream." It was a comfort just to hear the words, to remind herself that a civilized world existed, and she would get back to it one day. "Pedicure with Sea Salt and Rosemary Footbath and Aro…no, wait a minute—sea salt and rosemary—isn't that the flavouring of those organic chips I love? You'd probably like them," she confided to the little goat.

The little goat contentedly considered the proposition.

Noor tossed another brick into the salvage pile. Whoever had been assigned the task of destroying the few modest little homes that had once graced this clearing among the trees had done no more than knock them down and put a torch to the ruins, but though Noor and

Bari had searched diligently in the wreckage, they had found almost nothing, apart from the half-burned bricks, worth salvaging.

The inhabitants must have taken everything of any use with them when they were moved out—or maybe the people sent to destroy it had scavenged the site.

A rusted axe with a partially burned handle was their biggest prize so far, but the fire-blackened material that had once formed walls was very useful in their own building projects, and Bari was happy with that.

Noor, however, still had hopes.

"Please, God, just one little sliver of real soap!" she begged, returning to her work quickly, because the sun was getting higher and soon it would be too hot. There was no point in slacking, because Bari needed this stuff for the toilet he was now building.

She was working at the outer edge of the little village, where the fire hadn't burned so fiercely and the remains of a shattered house promised good pickings. With difficulty, using the stout stick Bari had found for her, Noor heaved up a sheet of corrugated iron. That would probably be very useful, but she wouldn't get it back to the campsite on her own. Bari would have to come and help.

Underneath was a piece of wood almost untouched by fire. Noor shifted the sheet to one side and let it fall, dragging her sarong up to cover her mouth and nose from the inevitable dust and soot thus stirred up. Then she bent and looked more closely at her find. It must be the door of the little house, and hardly touched by fire!

With a cry of excitement that had once been reserved for finds in designer sales, Noor snatched up her stick again and poked it under the board, moving it back and forth to scare off any snakes that might have taken up residence there. Then she levered the board upright.

Then she stopped, breathless, staring down at the flattened earth that had once been a family's living space…to the little rag doll that lay sprawled and abandoned there.

Noor's hand was trembling as she reached down to pick it up. She let the board fall back into place as she gazed at her discovery.

People were so outraged. International outcry.

The little doll was homemade, from a long sock stuffed with wadding. So simple, she noted absently. The toe is the head, the heel is the bum, slit the fabric from the top edge of the sock to the heel and stitch into legs. Make two arms with a bit of leftover fabric and stuffing and attach to the body under the head.

And with loving care, watched by an eager child, turn this basic shape into a personality with neatly embroidered black wool eyes, a smiling red mouth. Attach wool hair and braid thickly. Tie with a scrap of gold braid. Make a little floral-pattern tunic that matches the child's own dress.

Let the child dress and undress it, feed it and put it to bed, cuddle it and love it.

…Then, one dark day, it will fall unseen from the top of a hastily packed box of your precious belongings, or from the arm of the child, screaming because she sees her parents frightened and powerless as you are dragged from your home by brutal, uncaring strangers.

Noor could see the scene, could almost hear the shouts, the terrified wailing of children, the pleading of women, as if the anguish had imprinted itself into the little doll, into the broken bits of wood and brick, on the air, into the very earth.

Humanitarian outrage. Until this moment they had

been only words to her, and she realized it with shame. Noor Ashkani had always been quite sure she had a conscience. She gave to charity as religion dictated, and even went so far as to think the division of the world's riches unfair.

But as for real understanding…

"Why can't I go?" She could hear her own sulky voice arguing with her father, and remembered with deep, pulsing shame that when the resort on the main island had opened a few years ago and several of her wealthier friends had returned with stories of a holiday in heaven—she had wanted to vacation here.

Her father had put his foot down. That had been long before the international outcry had started, but he had tried to tell her the truth. Noor had sulked for weeks.

Now the human tragedy seemed to clutch at Noor's heart, as if with the child's desperate hands. The people to whom this had happened were her own people, but they were not alone in their suffering. She wondered how many ordinary people over the course of the past hundred years had been driven out of their ancestral homelands—by one means or another—in order to create playgrounds for the wealthy. Or military bases. Or cattle pasture. Or dust bowls.

And she herself was no better than a vandal now, scrabbling through the wreck of human lives for something to make her own life more comfortable.

To hell with it. Bari could be as scathing as he liked— she wasn't doing any more scavenging today. Noor dusted off the little doll as best she could, straightened its stained, mouldy dress, picked up her stick, wiped her eyes, and ran away from the wretched sound and stench of human misery created by other humans in the name of greed.

Noor returned to the campsite laden with fresh palm leaves to line the floor of their shelter, expecting to find Bari working.

But he wasn't there. The almost completed hut at the edge of the forest was deserted. So was the toilet, further in among the trees. His tools were flung down haphazardly in the sand, and a burned board he had been attaching hung askew.

Anxiety gripped her. Bari was methodical in his building, neat and precise with his few precious tools. What could have caused him to simply toss his work aside like this? Noor dropped her load and left the protection of the trees to look down the beach.

A few yards away, tossed in a heap, lay the weatherfaded white djellaba and rope she had made for him. Noor gazed along the beach, then out over the water. It was a moment before she noticed the flotsam that was spread over a broad area, being carried towards the island.

She gasped in mingled surprise, excitement, and fright. Did this represent a wrecked ship, or only a cargo lost overboard? What was in those boxes and crates?

The sea sparkled in the afternoon sunshine, lifting its tainted offering in a brilliant, tantalizing dance.

Might there be soap? Food? *Chocolate?*

From where she stood, she could see a large crate, a plastic-wrapped cardboard box, a cluster of rope, and dozens of lusciously bright, merrily bobbing oranges. It was probably only a matter of time before it all washed up on the beach, but Noor wouldn't be waiting for the tide. She untied her sarong and dropped it at her feet. The teddy was getting more frayed every day, but it served well enough for a swimsuit.

It was only as she was plunging into the water that

she saw the rest. Further along the bay, another cluster of boxes and crates was heading towards the rocks. Noor stood for a blank moment, staring. The surf was rough around the rocks. It was probably a hopeless task. And dangerous, if she got caught in an undertow.

And it might not even be worth it.

But in a choice between things that would probably come ashore on an accessible beach without her intervention, and rescuing what would otherwise be smashed against the rocks…

Where was Bari? Had he seen this? Biting her lip, her hand shading her eyes, Noor gazed up and down the beach, out over the water, hoping for some sign of him.

"Baaaari!" she called. "Baaareeee!"

No answer.

She turned and looked again at the precious cargo being driven towards the rocks. For the first time she didn't have Bari to tell her what to do. Should she go after those boxes, or was it too risky? And how? Most looked too big and cumbersome for her to simply grab hold of and then swim home.

Maybe it was a hopeless task. Maybe she should just wait and drag in the stuff that came right to this beach, make sure it landed safely.

But—

Making up her mind abruptly, Noor turned and ran to the life raft, where they kept their supplies, and snatched up a coil of nylon rope. Slinging it over her shoulder, she ran along the beach towards the rocks as far as possible, then went into the water and struck out for the nearest item.

It was a difficult and frustrating task. First she had to get the rope around the thing and tie it snugly, which was less easy than she'd have guessed. Then she had to get back to the beach. Noor had never engaged in a real struggle with nature, but now she became immersed in it, fighting the capricious sea for possession of the bounty it had brought so tantalizingly close.

She heaved a sigh of exhausted triumph as she landed a small wooden crate safely, untied the rope and immediately went back in the water for another. It was then that she saw Bari in the water, much further out, grappling with a large crate. She had no idea how long he had been there.

After that, there was only the burning heat, the painful glare and sparkle of sunlight on water, the wrenching discomfort in her arms and back and legs as she pulled and pushed, dancing out of the way when the surf suddenly bounced a crate along the sand, returning to the struggle the moment she had one safely landed.

"Noor!"

She looked up, out of a dream, unsure how much time had passed. The beach was littered with salvage. She had been vaguely aware of Bari dragging a chain of smallish items ashore at least once—he tied several pieces to the rope and then landed them all together.

She looked around. He was in the water, well out from shore.

"Throw me your rope!"

There was something in his voice that compelled instant response. Her heart kicked as she dragged the rope from the box she had nearly beached. She coiled the rope as she dashed back into the water and half ran, half swam in Bari's direction.

"Don't come any further!"

The sunlight was dancing on the ripples, painfully bright and beautiful. Bari's arm was outstretched in the water, his fist gripping the end of his rope. At the other end was a cluster of three crates. The water had already dragged them to the fullest extent of the rope, and she could see that he was exhausted with the struggle to hold them.

"Stand firm, hold one end tight and throw me the other end," he ordered calmly.

Something was wrong. Noor gasped, her heart pushing into her throat. A sense of danger and threat seemed to fill the air.

"Bari!" she shrieked. "Let it go!"

"Throw it!"

She gripped her rope with shaking fingers. "Leave it, Bari—whatever it is, it's not worth it!"

If he was dragged toward the rocks, caught in the surf—

"Throw the damned rope!"

With a prayer for strength, Noor tossed the curl of rope in a backhander like her best tennis swing. It snaked out, painting a long grey line in the air before landing with a soundless splash a few yards from him.

She could see the other rope pulling him from his target.

"It's too dangerous!" she screamed. "Let it go!"

His arms stretched to their fullest extent, he at last snatched up the rope she had tossed. Then he lifted the other rope end, and against the buffeting of the waves, she saw, was struggling to drag the other rope closer in order to tie her rope to the one that held the packages. But the drag on the packages was too strong, and he was being constantly buffeted by waves.

She couldn't give him any more rope without getting drawn into the breakers. Already she was being dragged along the beach towards the rocks; she was knocked almost off her feet when a bigger wave caught Bari and he went under.

"Bari, it won't reach!" she screamed. "Let go of the crates!"

If he was dragged against the rocks, he would be so badly smashed up—why didn't he let the damned crates go?

The weight suddenly eased and Noor saw the three crates sailing away, the end of the white rope curling and swirling in a little eddy. Relief flowed through her so hot her knees almost buckled.

"Oh, thank God, thank God!"

"Can you pull me in?" Bari called.

He worked his way towards the sandy beach at an angle, not fighting the current directly. Slowly he got away from the rocks, while Noor, keeping a tight grip on the rope, dragged him in. It was a little like reeling in a wild stallion.

When he stood up out of the waves at last, staggered towards her and then fell again, she saw blood streaming from a long gash in his thigh.

Twelve

He was heavy, almost a dead weight on her, and that terrified her. Bari wasn't a man to show weakness, but he was leaning on her hard, grimacing with every step, dragging the wounded leg as if unable to put any weight on it at all. His breath rasped in her ear, sending shivers of blank terror through her. If he was seriously wounded, what would happen to them?

She helped him up the beach to the little hut, where he sank down onto the foil sheet with a stifled groan. Gripped by horror, Noor stared helplessly at the long wound running down his thigh.

"Ya Allah!" she moaned, her mother's favourite expression in the face of trouble. Thoughts of infection, gangrene and amputation danced grotesquely across her imagination. How dreadful to think of him losing a leg, and all because she—

"First aid kit."

His voice was a whisper; he was clearly in pain. Noor came abruptly to her senses. He was the wounded one—he shouldn't have to do the organizing! But she was the only other person available.

She had to concentrate.

First aid kit. Noor ran to the overturned life raft, under which they stowed their equipment, scrabbled wildly for the first aid kit, then, from the diminishing pile of white silk she had salvaged from her carefully demolished wedding dress, grabbed a medium-sized square.

Back at the shelter, she knelt beside him. The bleeding was already slowing. At least he wasn't going to bleed to death! Her panic subsiding somewhat, she began to tear the silk into strips. Such basic action made her feel more competent and confident.

"I'm sure it needs stitches," she told Bari, though she had nothing more than television hospital dramas to go on.

"Never mind. The important thing is to get antiseptic onto it."

She was sure she should use boiled water to wash the wound first, but there was no possibility of that. Even if she had a pot to boil it in, she had already proved hopeless at lighting the fire.

The fire! They had lighted it every night for a signal, as well as the psychological and physical comfort it offered. But who would light it tonight?

"The drinking water in the emergency kit will be sterile," Bari said, sending her dashing back to the raft to search for some of the tiny little plastic packs of water which they hadn't had to touch yet.

What followed was the most nerve-racking half hour of her life. Under the patient's quiet but clear instructions she washed the ugly wound, made sure it was clean, bathed it with antiseptic, then drew the edges of the gash together, applied sterile pads, and taped them as neatly as she could. Then she bound his thigh with a clean bandage and, afterwards, strips of silk. Finally, to protect the bandages, she wrapped and taped a plastic bag around the whole.

"Does it feel all right?" she asked at last.

"It feels fine. Thank you," Bari said, still breathing in a way that frightened her. "You made a very work-manlike job of it."

Even though she knew it wasn't true—some of her taping looked like a five-year-old's craft project—Noor was swept with an unfamiliar sense of accomplishment. She'd done it! She'd actually managed it! Something had desperately needed to be done, and, however inexpertly, she had done it!

"Thank you," she said, with real humility. She smiled down at Bari, feeling a strangely touching connection with him because she had been able to help. "I'm really glad I could do it."

"So am I."

After all the cynical looks in the past, his approving smile now was like rain on new roots. They gazed into each other's eyes for a moment of silence. In the forest the birds began to sing the sun down.

"Do you want a painkiller?"

"No," said Bari. His mouth contorted. "Yes."

She pressed a tablet out of the bubble pack and gave it to him with a little water. He drank it and lay back with a little grunt of pain.

"How did it happen?"

"I didn't see whatever it was. I was kicking hard against the current and it was in my way. A jutting rock, maybe."

Her breath hissed in sympathy. "Do you—" She blew her breath up over her forehead, sending a tendril of hair dancing. "Is it broken?"

He was silent for a moment. "No. The bone may be bruised. It'll be a day or two at most before I can put weight on it."

She wasn't sure she believed that. Might he be lying to keep her calm, or was he maybe in a state of denial?

"*Ya Allah,*" Noor whispered again, her eyes wide, as the full extent of what his injury would mean began to unfold in her mind.

"Tomorrow you'll collect some herbs for me. Good thing the shelter is nearly done," he muttered drowsily. Reaction was setting in. "You'll be able to manage."

Manage! She stared at him in mute protest. Bari's eyelids fluttered, and Noor's heart fluttered in response. If he lost consciousness—! The weight of the world seemed to be on her shoulders all at once.

"Bari! Do you want anything?" she cried, just to see him open his eyes again. To know that he could.

He took a long time to collect his thoughts, gazing at her with a frown. Then he shook his head.

"Do we have any food?"

At the mention of the word her stomach growled. Because of the salvage operation Bari hadn't gone fishing today. They hadn't foraged for eggs. The sun was very low now. Behind her, the birdsong was at its evening peak. She would have little chance of finding anything in the dark.

"There are dates," she remembered, getting to her feet. She had laid some dates out in the sun in the hopes of drying them.

But as she stepped out of the shelter, she stopped short. "The salvage! I forgot all about it!" she cried jubilantly.

She dashed back inside the shelter and snatched up the little knife.

"Take it easy with that thing," Bari protested.

But Noor barely heard. A moment later she was half-way along the beach, bending over one of the biggest boxes. The slanting sun picked out the delicate Arabic letters she had not had time to examine before.

"'Al Bostan luxury food importers!'" she translated with a happy shout. "Food! I knew it!" With hands made clumsy by excitement, hunger, and fatigue, she finally managed to slit the plastic packaging, and then the packing tape. Eagerly she pulled up the cardboard flaps.

In the sunshine the cellophane-wrapped packages were unmistakable. Her heart lifted with crazy joy.

"Lettuce!" she shrieked, as excited as, in a former life, she might have cried *Moët et Chandon!*

She reached in and drew one head of lettuce out of the neatly packed box. Then she glanced back towards the shelter and frowned a little. Wilted lettuce. Not exactly the meal of choice for an invalid.

"I suppose the tinned soup went straight to the bottom," she muttered darkly, as if the soup would regret that choice one day.

She chose a smaller box and renewed her attack, much more proficient with the knife than she would have been even a few days ago, if she had been in a state of mind to notice….

It was like a joke, but somehow Noor couldn't laugh. She had half killed herself, and Bari had ripped up and maybe broken his leg, and all they had to show for it was…

"What's that howling?" she heard from the shelter. She got up and walked over to where he lay.

"Two boxes opened so far," she reported in a flat voice. "And the score—we are now in proud possession of two dozen severely wilted heads of romaine lettuce and a few thousand plastic swizzle sticks."

A shout of laughter met her ears as she dropped one of each on the ground beside him.

She laughed with him. It was that or cry.

Bari picked up the swizzle stick and frowned at it in the fading light. "I thought so," he said after a moment, and held it up. "See the logo? The shipment was destined for the Gulf Eden Resort. They bring fresh food and supplies over from the mainland on a daily basis. One of the dhows either sank or had to cut loose the cargo during the storm."

"It's taken a long time to beach, hasn't it?" Noor asked.

Bari shrugged. "The currents among the islands can be very difficult, particularly after a storm. Every sailor learns that quickly. And that blow we had last night might have had something to do with it." Last night there had been a horrible wind and high rough seas smashing up the beach. "The wooden crates may contain less perishable food," he suggested.

"From your lips to God's ears!" Noor said, reaching for the axe and hefting it like a pro. She scarcely noticed how the burned handle blackened her callused hands.

A little later Noor stumbled up the beach into the hut with her arms full. She dropped to her knees beside Bari and spilled the riches on the sand.

"It's really hard to prise open those crates!" she cried. Her hands were bruised, bleeding and filthy, but she was exultant.

"But you managed?" Bari asked.

"Two of them, plus a couple of the boxes, and I've got the knack now— I can do the others tomorrow!" Noor said jubilantly. "And look what I found!"

"What?" He smiled at her, and Noor blinked on an in-drawn breath. She had never seen quite that expression in his eyes before, and somehow it made her heart skip.

"*Ta da!* Smoked salmon!" she cried, holding it up, too excited to save the best till last.

"What a relief to know the civilized world still exists."

"It's food, isn't it?" Noor said defensively, reacting to the irony. "I love smoked salmon, and we've got *pounds* of it, in packs that are good for *years!*"

Bari laughed, his eyes alight with that strange warmth. "I did say we might be stranded for a while, but I hope…"

She was too focused to appreciate his irony. "I know, Bari, but the point is, it's good for as long as we need it. It's good now. Not like the lettuce."

"*Alhamdolillah,*" he said.

"And rice! Bags of it. Who'd have thought that would float? And water biscuits, and a huge carton of potato chips, look, and—" she scrabbled happily among her treasures "—oh, and *coffee!* Isn't that just *so* fantastic? I'm almost crazy for a cup of coffee!"

"All we need now is the cup," he teased.

"And a pot for boiling the water! I haven't found anything useful like that yet, but there must be some way to make something that'll work."

She didn't see the expression that crossed his face. "You think so?"

"Not everything was for the hotel kitchens. There's some stock for different boutiques. Haven't you no-ticed?" She lifted a hand and struck a pose.

"You have a new forage cap," he said admiringly.

"Not just any forage cap, either! This is the last word in desert chic." Noor turned her head to display the can-vas flap that protected her neck, as if she were a member of the French Foreign Legion. "Notice the discreet Gulf Eden Resort logo! Only the truly discerning—well, the obscenely rich—will recognize that, of course."

"Of course," Bari agreed gravely.

"I'll bet the shop sells bikinis to match, too! I'd love it if I found one. This thing I'm wearing is just about at the end of its very short but traumatic life span. But it'll be dark soon—I had to stop. How hungry are you for dinner?"

"Homicidal," Bari allowed with a grin.

"Smoked salmon and crackers?"

Noor had cut little squares from the plastic that sealed the boxes, which now she laid over pieces of board chopped from a crate, to serve as plates.

She peeled open a pack of smoked salmon and a box of water biscuits, poured water into their one plastic cup and set it carefully in the sand, then sat back, as proud and satisfied as if she had produced a five-course meal.

"Doesn't that look delicious?" she cried, her stomach growling in anticipation.

"Best offer I've had all day," Bari agreed.

They fell on the food as if it were a feast. "Oh, the taste of *salt!* And who'd have believed a simple cracker could be so satisfying?" Noor demanded, munching, when they had demolished most of the meal in silence.

Bari nodded, picked up the cup of water, and offered it to her.

As she reached to take it, Noor suddenly noticed her hands. She always scrubbed her hands with sand and seawater at the end of every day, not with much success. But tonight she had been too busy. Dirt was packed around the ragged nails, the callused palms were black with soot from the axe handle, the skin of her fingers raw and scraped with the effort of opening the crates.

She shrugged. Well, she had worked hard, and it was no surprise if her hands showed it. As her fingers closed around the little cup, she felt a curious pride, as though the dirt of hard work were a badge that marked her kinship with women all over the globe, the women who wrest a living from the earth.

Suddenly she felt how much she deserved the drink. For the first time in her life, Noor unconsciously made the connection between work and self-worth. Always before, she had been given whatever she needed by right. Because her father was rich, because she was who she was.

Today she had earned the food she had eaten, and this drink of water, and she felt the difference.

They were lying together in the shelter, with a foil sheet over them. Noor was restless and couldn't sleep, but there was absolutely nothing she could do to amuse herself. The darkness was intense, she had discovered, when there was no city glow to lighten it.

She sighed unhappily. For the past three days, everything had fallen on her. Bari said his leg was improving daily, but he still couldn't stand on it for longer than a few minutes at a time, so he wasn't doing much in the way of work.

He could give her instruction and advice, though, and Noor was learning fast. She had learned to light a fire, though not without first wasting too much of the fuel in the little cigarette lighter. She had even caught a fish in the net Bari had made from her wedding veil and a pliant branch. With nothing but his verbal description to go by, she had found the right healing herb in the forest, and made a paste to put on his wounds.

Nearly every day new packets from the lost cargo

washed up on the beach, and every day she invented new uses for frustratingly useless artefacts from a way of life which seemed increasingly distant and incomprehensible.

She had constructed a backgammon game for them. For counters, from the dozens of tiny fridge magnets she found in one package, she had chosen fifteen bearing a miniature Old Palace, and another fifteen of the Great Mosque. The board she created out of the cardboard box itself, outlined the points with Bari's knife, and then stained alternate points with crushed berries.

She had brought Bari small bits of dried wood and instructed him to carve them into dice. In the evenings, when darkness descended, they lay by the fire, playing while the flame faded to glowing ash.

On an impulse she couldn't resist, Noor had threaded the pearls from her wedding dress onto a piece of fishing line, and made a necklace, first for herself, and then for the little rag doll she had found, whom she had named Laqiya. Bari had admired them both with apparently equal approval.

This morning she had opened a huge box addressed to a boutique in the resort called MemorArabia to find a half dozen replica beaten brass bowls and a couple of large replica hookahs, all wrapped in enough plastic bubble wrap to build a tent. The hookahs she had set aside with a snort of contempt. "What would anybody want with them?" she demanded indignantly. "What *use* would they be?"

Bari laughed. "It's a good thing you don't work in the tourism industry."

"But what a *waste!* I mean, someone will take that home and put it on their mantelpiece and it'll collect dust for three months and then be given to charity, and someone else will take it home and put it on their coffee table, and that's its story. It's excellent quality—I bet it's a functioning hookah—but who's ever going to smoke it? And look at all the materials that have gone into it! This is real brass tubing. It could have been…"

With a little indrawn breath, Noor fell silent. And a couple of hours later, she had extracted the tubing from several hookahs and mounted it over the fire, supported by stones at each end. On the little platform thus created she put a replica beaten brass bowl from the same shop, and so boiled water for the first time.

"Coffee!" she sang as she stirred the powder into the steaming water. Her ladle was the plastic cup from the emergency kit, and she carefully decanted several measures of the hot coffee into another brass bowl and offered it to Bari, before doing the same for herself.

"Isn't that heaven?" she demanded as the scent teased her nostrils and she waited for the liquid to cool. "I feel as though I grew the stuff and ground it myself!"

Maybe it was the coffee that stopped her sleeping now, she reflected. After so long with no caffeine, it might have had an effect on her that it didn't use to have. She was utterly exhausted by the day's work, so what other explanation could there be?

She wished she could snuggle up against Bari, but although they slept close under the same foil sheet, he never offered to actually hold her. Sometimes when she awoke, it was to discover that she had wormed her way into his embrace in her sleep, but she had never done it in cold blood.

His breathing told her he was awake, too. Her pride had taken a bad beating when she'd discovered his true opinion of her, and although their relationship had now improved out of all recognition, she was still nervous of what his reaction would be if she asked him to hold her. She had asked him once before and been harshly repulsed, and the humiliation was ever fresh.

In the darkness she felt him fold his arms under his head. "Can't sleep?" he murmured softly.

"No. Isn't it ridiculous? Every muscle is screaming for a rest, too." Belatedly she remembered that he had even more reason to complain. "What about you? Is it pain that's keeping you awake?"

He grunted without answering, and she supposed he felt it was unmanly to admit to suffering.

"Do you think your leg is healing properly?"

He didn't answer, and Noor felt a shiver of dread. What would she do if he suffered complications? What if the wound became infected? The mess of herbs he had asked her to apply to the wound had looked positively toxic, and she didn't have even first aid training, let alone any medical qualifications.

"If we ever get out of this, I'm going to take a first aid course," she vowed fervently. "And I'm going to get some kind of practical training in something, too."

Bari was silent for so long she wondered if he'd fallen asleep. But then, in an odd voice, he asked, "What sort of practical training?"

"I don't know yet. I'll have to look around. Plumbing, maybe!" She laughed a little. "Something useful. You know, Bari, it's like—here we are on a desert island, and only certain skills count. And only certain things are useful, and the useless things are just so much garbage clogging up our campsite—and the island. And it's what you said—there's no room for anyone who doesn't pull their weight, and if we don't cooperate, we die. But you know what I've just realized?"

"What?"

"The whole world is a desert island. It's no different than what we've got right here. It's just—easier to overlook the truth out there."

There was another long pause, but this time she knew he had heard.

"I see," he said softly.

"So when we get back—*will* we ever get back?—I want to start doing something useful. Something like engineering, or medicine, or…I wonder if it's too late to start. Do you think I'm being silly?"

"No," he said softly. "Why would I think it silly to want to make a contribution to the world?"

Noor laughed in sudden recognition. "That's what it is, isn't it? I hadn't thought of it just like that!" She laughed again. "*Ya Allah,* I've become a do-gooder! Do you think I'll turn into a poor-little-rich-girl who runs around orphanages wringing her hands?"

Bari laughed, too. "Not unless you want to."

"Well, I don't. I want to do something *practical*."

"From the evidence of the past few days, you might consider becoming an inventor," he offered, only half joking.

Noor was silent, absorbing that. "I think that's the biggest compliment I've ever had," she said softly.

And it was in that strangely sweet moment that she realized she did love him, after all. Had she loved him from that first moment? Had her own self-absorption simply hidden the truth from her? Or was it only since she had come to the island that her heart had opened enough to let love in? She couldn't say when the seed had been planted, but the full-blown plant was unmistakable.

She had a terrible, powerful urge to tell him so, but fear stopped her. He had pretended to love her when in his heart he felt contempt. And his reasons for marrying her hadn't changed: he still wanted to please his grandfather. He wanted to inherit the family estates.

If she told him of her love, would he pretend to love her again? She was almost certain that he liked her better now, but what if he didn't?

Noor was feeling desperately confused all at once, and she shifted restlessly. "Oh, what I'd give for a portable DVD player and a good movie!" She cried out her frustration in the darkness.

"Is that what you normally do when you can't sleep?"

"I don't have much trouble sleeping usually, but when I do, yes, I get up and watch a movie. Or read. Or write e-mails to my friends. That's the problem with technology—where is it when you really need it?" She laughed, her heart stretched with pain and confusion, when she wanted to weep. "I wonder what primitive cultures do for insomnia?"

"The same, only without the technology," he suggested. "Would you like me to tell you a story?"

Noor gave a little grunt of surprise. "My father always used to tell me stories! I'd almost forgotten. Does your story have jinns and fairies and giant rocs?"

"Of course." Her heart beat with sudden urgency as she felt him lift an arm and offer to slide it under her head. Wordlessly Noor slipped up to rest on his bare shoulder as his arm drew her in against him.

"Is your leg comfortable?"

"It's fine," Bari said mildly. "Now be quiet and listen."

Thirteen

"**O**nce upon a time, there was a king who had an exceedingly beautiful daughter, named Zarsana. The girl was so beautiful, and so sweet natured, that everyone said she could hardly be human. Among themselves the servants called her the Fairy Princess. She was the joy of both her father and her mother.

"One day, the King said to the Queen, 'Although it will pain us to lose her, it is time that our daughter was married. We must find her a suitable husband. In our pleasure in her company we have already delayed too long.'

"The next day, the King visited his daughter in her rooms in the palace, and told her his thoughts. But Princess Zarsana smiled at her father and said, 'Why should I leave you and my mother when we are so happy as we are? Do not seek to change things, but let us remain together.'

"Her father insisted that it was the fate of every young

woman to marry, and at last the Princess said, 'I will marry only a man who has visited the City of Gold.'

"Her father was astonished, for he had never heard of the City of Gold. He tried to dissuade his daughter, but the Princess was adamant. At last the King went away and consulted with his viziers.

"None of the viziers, not even the Grand Vizier, had ever heard of the Golden City. But as ignorance never holds back an expert, they consulted together and advised the King.

"'You must invite all the eligible princes of the world to visit, and ask which of them has seen the City of Gold,' they advised. 'Whoever says he has made such a trip shall marry the Princess.'

"But when the King invited all the princes of the world and asked each of them in turn if he had visited the City of Gold, none had even heard of the place. And they all returned to their homes none the wiser regarding the reason of the visit.

"Then the viziers said, 'Your Cup Companions are all men of the highest nobility. Ask them whether any has succeeded in visiting the Golden City, and whoever says he has shall marry your daughter.'

"So the King ordered a feast, to which he summoned his Cup Companions. When they had eaten and drunk, recited poetry and discussed philosophy and love in the usual way, the King spoke.

"'Which of you has visited the City of Gold? For whoever has done so shall marry my daughter, Zarsana, and I will make him Crown Prince.'

"Of course all the Cup Companions wished very much for such a fate, for Zarsana's beauty and good nature were well-known, and whoever was Crown Prince would inherit the kingdom in the course of time. But each had to confess that he had never even heard of such a place as the Golden City.

"When the King summoned his viziers again, they scratched their heads. 'No other man can be sufficiently noble to marry the Princess, even if he has seen the Golden City,' they agreed. 'The Princess must give up her determination to marry such a man.' And they had no more advice to offer.

"So the King paid a visit to the Princess again, and explained the difficulty. 'No one has even heard of the City of Gold. How is such a man to be found? You must give up your determination and let me choose a husband for you.'

"But the girl refused.

"'Let a proclamation be made in the streets,' advised Princess Zarsana. 'Say that I will marry that man, whatever his birth or rank, who has visited the Golden City.'

"The worried King did as his daughter had instructed, and messengers were sent out into the city to announce that whoever had seen the City of Gold should travel to the palace, where he would marry the Princess Zarsana and be made Crown Prince.

"The announcement caused great excitement in the kingdom, and the news was passed from lip to lip, but not even the oldest of the King's subjects had ever heard of such a place as the Golden City.

"At last the news came to the ears of a handsome young man named Salik, the son of a silk merchant who had died leaving his son enormously rich. Salik had squandered all his father's wealth on gambling and vice, and now he was very miserable. His false friends had abandoned him when they saw that all his money was gone, and he was too ashamed to approach any of his father's old friends in his present state.

"When he heard the proclamation, Salik said to himself, 'Since no one knows of this city, who will be able to challenge me if I say I have seen it? This is the way to mend my fortunes, for I can sink no lower than I already am.' So he went to the palace and said to the guards, 'I am the man the King seeks. I have visited the City of Gold and seen it with my own eyes.'

"Salik was taken before the King, to whom he repeated the false claim. The King in turn sent him to the Princess. Princess Zarsana said to Salik, 'Have you seen the Golden City?' 'Yes,' replied Salik. 'While I was on my travels in search of knowledge, I reached the City of Gold.' 'And by what route did you travel there?' she asked.

"Salik was undaunted. 'From my home in this city I travelled for many days, till I came to the great city of Isfahan. From there I made my way through the Dasht-i Kavir, and after great struggles found my way to Zanzibar. From there I went to Bokhara, and thence to Samarkand. From Samarkand through the mountains, I made my way to the shores of the sea. I entered the City of Gold, which is as beautiful as paradise. There I studied for many months, and at last made my way home.'

"The Princess smiled. 'What you tell me is wonderful, and it is clear that you have indeed seen the Golden City. Tell me again how you travelled there.'

"Feeling pleased with his success, Salik began to embroider.

"'From here I journeyed with great difficulties to Isfahan, and from there I joined a caravan through the Dasht-i Kavir. In Zanzibar I left the caravan and travelled with a friend to Samarkand, and what adventures we met with along the way I shall entertain you with at a later date. In Bokhara I met a wise man, who gave me advice and directed my footsteps through the mountains to the Golden City.'

"The Princess ordered her servants to throw Salik out into the street, and when her father came to ask after him, she chided him for not realizing that the young man was a rogue. 'Do not be impatient, Father,' she advised. 'For this may take time.' So the King ordered that the crier should walk the streets of the city every day, making the announcement that any man who had visited the City of Gold would marry the Princess.

"But as for Salik, he was in very low spirits. He was now in a much worse case than before, for not only had he lied and been found out, earning everyone's contempt, but at his first sight of her he had fallen deeply in love with the Princess. And he had failed to win her.

"The young man wandered for some time, bewailing his fate and regretting the Princess. At last he decided that, as he could not live without her as his wife, he must do what was necessary to win her. He made up his mind to go through the world, searching for the City of Gold until he found it, or died in the attempt.

"So Salik set out on his journey, and travelled until he reached the forest of Aghaz, which was home to wild animals and robbers, and which seemed to extend before the traveller, however fast he moved. Salik journeyed through the forest, and at length came to a tree under which a very ancient dervish was living. The hermit welcomed him and served him with food and drink, and asked where he was going. Salik told the dervish of his quest, but the dervish could not tell him anything of the City of Gold. He sent Salik to his older brother, who was also a hermit, in far distant mountains.

"But the sage of the mountain also had not heard of

the Golden City. He in his turn advised Salik to travel
to the seashore, and thence to a far distant island in the
ocean, named Jariza. Jariza was ruled by a rich foreign
king, Ashabi, who was known for his foreign travels,
and who might know of the City of Gold.

"So Salik proceeded to the seashore, where he ob-
tained passage to Jariza with a merchant ship. But when
the ship had almost reached its destination, a black
storm blew up, and the ship, lashed by winds and waves
as high as mountains, broke up. Salik and the merchant
were tossed into the sea, and Salik was immediately
swallowed whole by a giant fish.

"Soon after, the fish was captured by fishermen, and
because it was so big, they took it as a wonder to the
King of their country. In the King's presence the giant
fish was cut open, and to everyone's amazement, a handsome young man emerged.

"At the King's enquiry, Salik introduced himself and
explained his mission. 'And now,' he finished, 'I am on
my way to the court of King Ashabi of the island kingdom of Jariza, for he is a great traveller and seafarer, and
he may know of the City of Gold.'

"The King laughed in amazement and said, 'I am
Ashabi, and this island is Jariza,' and everyone was astonished at this outcome of the fishermen's gift.

"The King had heard of the City of Gold as being sit-
uated on a far distant island, but he did not know where.
But on an island not far away there was a shrine, and to
that shrine, in a week's time, would come pilgrims from
all over the islands. The King offered to take Salik to
the pilgrimage, in order that he might question the pilgrims about the City of Gold.

"So Salik remained with the King until the time
came, and then they set sail for the shrine. But as they

voyaged, they passed an island on which stood a giant tree with a thick trunk and broad, low-hanging branches. Salik asked King Ashabi about the tree, but the King said, 'We dare not approach closer, for there is a great whirlpool which lets go of no boat once it has been trapped.' And just at that moment they felt the boat tremble beneath them; the whirlpool had captured the boat. As the boat was drawn into the vortex, it came closer and closer to the island and the giant tree. Salik was able to leap up and pull himself up into the branches of the tree. There he hid himself, watching the boat disappear into the whirlpool, and wondering what to do.

"When night fell, a flock of giant rocs came to roost in the tree, and Salik discovered he could understand their speech. The rocs were discussing their activities of the day and their plans for the morrow. After some time, one of them said to the others, 'Today I have feasted in the Golden City, and tomorrow I will do the same, for the gardens are so lush there I see no reason to travel further.'

"Salik was elated to hear this, and when the rocs were fast asleep, he climbed up onto the back of the one who had spoken of the City of Gold, and hid himself in his feathers. In the morning the roc flew to the Golden City and alighted in a beautiful garden.

"Salik slipped from his back undetected and wandered about the garden until he met two women. He asked them what the place was, and the women told him that it was the City of Gold, ruled by a fairy princess named Perizan for her sister, Queen Marifa, who was absent, and that they were the Queen's gardeners.

"They conducted the traveller to the palace and into the presence of the Princess, who asked him for his story. When he had told her everything, Princess Perizan said, 'Your story interests me very much and I would like to know more. However, I must go with my women on a visit that cannot be delayed. I shall be away two days. You will be comfortable here in the palace—order whatever you wish. But on no account go into the Inner Pavilion.'

"With that, Perizan and her women departed, leaving Salik to wander through the beautiful palace and its magnificent gardens. He was delighted, for the palace was the most wonderful thing he had ever seen, with pillars glittering with precious stones, and walls of beaten gold. In the gardens grew plants the like of which he had never seen, of enchanting beauty, visited by birds of brilliant hue and thrilling song. Whatever he asked for was brought to him instantly, and the food was flavoured with spices so delicious every meal was an enchantment.

"But on the afternoon of the second day, as is the way of mortals, he began to wonder why the Princess had forbidden him the Inner Pavilion. And at length the young man's curiosity overwhelmed him, and he made his way to the central courtyard of the palace, where the Inner Pavilion stood in its own lush garden, its golden dome glowing like a sun. Salik climbed the staircase and found himself on a broad terrace encircling a glittering pagoda that was composed of sweeping arches and the domed roof, all studded with mirrors and laced with gold. In the centre of the pagoda was an eight-sided chamber. And in one of the sides, Salik saw a door.

"When he opened the door he found himself in a chamber even more beautifully and richly decorated than all that had preceded it. The walls glowed from the sparkle of a million diamonds, and were hung with pictures painted with rubies, emeralds, sapphires, turquoises, amethysts, and a strange jewel, black as ebony, that glittered like a serpent's eye.

"Eight arched windows carved into the domed roof let in a mysterious light that fell upon a divan resting upon a raised dais in the centre of the chamber. The divan was covered with magnificent cloth of gold embroidered all over with diamonds and pearls.

"It covered the form of a beautiful woman, who lay absolutely still. Her black hair cascaded down behind her to the floor like a curtain, threaded with gold, in each curl a perfect pearl. In the centre of her forehead a large diamond on a band of woven gold seemed to capture all the mysterious light from the windows and send it flashing out to every corner of the chamber.

"Salik shielded his eyes from the bright rays and, as if hypnotized, approached the sleeping woman to look down at her face. With amazed bewilderment, he beheld the form of his beloved, the Princess Zarsana, whom he had seen in the palace so many months before.

"He called to her, but could not rouse her. Not knowing whether she was sleeping, dead, or merely an image, Salik wandered disconsolately out of the chamber to sit on the terrace overlooking the garden and consider, trying to make sense of what he had seen.

"He looked down into the garden and discovered a lake he had not noticed before. Beside the lake was a magnificently caparisoned horse, whose coat was black as the night sky, bearing a richly jewelled saddle of red gold, but without a bridle. Blinking in wonderment, Salik descended into the garden and approached the horse. But when he tried to mount it, the horse kicked him, so hard that he was sent into the centre of the lake. Salik sank under the surface, and when he rose again, he discovered that he was in the lake of a garden in his own city.

"Troubled and astonished, Salik emerged from the lake and left the garden. And as he walked the familiar streets, wondering what had happened to him and whether it had all been a dream, he heard the town crier beating the drum and announcing, 'Whoever has seen the City of Gold will marry the Princess and become the Crown Prince.'

"Immediately he went to the palace and said to the guards, 'I have seen the Golden City. Take me to the King.'

"The guards led Salik to the throne room, but when he was admitted to the King's presence, the Cup Companions and courtiers and viziers at once began to cry, 'This is the very villain who came before, and whom the Princess had thrown into the streets for his insolent lies!' And the King, too, remembered him, and threatened him with severe punishment if Salik persisted in his falseness.

"But, though frightened, Salik stood firm. 'Take me to the Princess,' he insisted, 'and if she rejects me again, I accept death as my fit punishment.'

"The King consulted with his viziers, but their advice was confused and contradictory, and for every one who advised one thing, another advised the opposite. And at last the King sent a message to the Princess Zarsana, who came to the throne room accompanied by her women.

"'Father, do you listen to more lies from such a rogue?' she asked the King.

"But Salik stepped forward and cried, 'Tell me how it is that I saw your lifeless form in the Inner Pavilion of the palace of the Golden City, and yet see you here alive!'

"Then the Princess smiled and, turning to the King again, said, 'He speaks the truth, and he will be my husband. But he will not become Crown Prince here in your kingdom, for he must return with me and live forever in the City of Gold.

"'Know that my true name is Marifa. I am Queen in my own land, and in my absence my sister rules in my stead. I was cursed to be born among mortals and live as one of you until a mortal man should, for love of me, visit the Golden City and see my true form there. Now he will become one of us and rule my kingdom with me. And he will henceforth be called Asheq, for his love is true.'

"And hard upon her words, the wonderful black horse flew in through one of the tall windows of the palace and came to rest in front of the Princess. Salik mounted the horse, with the Princess in front of him. And to the wonderment of all in the throne room, the horse mounted into the air and flew out of the window, all the way to the City of Gold.

"Queen Marifa and King Asheq arrived in the City of Gold amid great rejoicing, and they ruled there for many years, and Allah sent them peace and happiness."

Fourteen

His voice faded into silence, and they lay without speaking for a long moment. Then Noor said, "Thank you, that was lovely," in a drowsy, sensually charged voice, and it seemed the most natural thing in the world that Bari should lift his head and bend over her.

Her hand was pressed against his naked chest, half in fear, as deep, urgent need flowed through her. She licked her lips and her eyes tried to pierce the darkness to see his expression. But the last glow of the fire was almost gone, and the first light of the moon had yet to make its appearance.

"Noor," he murmured, in a voice that melted her, and when he felt the long, responsive sigh, his mouth came down and brushed her eyelid and her cheek in a tender quest for her mouth. Noor sighed as his lips teased and nibbled and at last took possession of hers, and of their own accord her arms slipped up to encircle his neck.

His hand pressed hard along the length of her back, and then he moved his fingers to the neckline of the jacket she wore, and slowly, expertly, began to unbutton it.

It was dark, they were guided by touch and scent alone, but still she saw a golden glow as his hand found her breast, and then his mouth lifted and laid a tracery of kisses down her throat, and she responded with hot melting as his tongue tasted her skin.

She kissed his neck, stroked his firmly muscled chest, cupped his head, feeling the silken curls cling around her fingers. Then her hand clenched as his touch shivered along her stomach and abdomen and he found his way unerringly to the nest of clustered nerves at her centre.

Pleasure poured through her, as if liquid gold shot from his fingers, and Noor told him her delight with low, panting cries of gratitude and release. She reached for him then, her hand enclosing his aroused flesh, and gasped a little breath of hungry recognition.

His skin was silken marble, warm and pulsing, and the cry that came from his throat was the sign of her female power, and melted her into fainting pleasure again. They stroked and pressed and kissed until the pleasure was like a madness. And then at last, with a rough groan, his hips slipped between her hungrily welcoming thighs, and his flesh into that place that had already become home to him.

He rose up above her, and behind his head the moon also climbed, gilding their lair with white-gold fingers, brushing his velvet curls, her forehead, her ear, as he moved in her. And for both of them the light seemed to enter their bodies, liquid pleasure that built with each stroke of him inside her, till they were blinded by the brightness, burned by its heat.

Then unbelievable pleasure forced its way through every vein, into every cell, and fountained up in her throat in a wild cry as free as the wildest animal's call. Over and over, down and down and down, pounding, grinding, the mortar and pestle of their bodies breaking the fresh herb of passion to produce the pure essence, the pungent rich oil of deep, immeasurable ecstasy.

The perfume of it burst through their being then, for they were in the world of separation no longer. "I love you," they heard on the air, half fainting, not knowing whether it was her throat or his, or Love itself, that formed the words. And there was no duality, no past and future, no I and Thou; there was only the One.

Bari stood at the water's edge, watching the first rays of the sun divide the black of the sea from the black of the heavens.

He was caught in his own trap. He had wanted to make her love him, and instead… He laughed in sound-less mockery at his blind hubris. A woman like her, vital, beautiful, with a quick intelligence and a heart now revealed as good and true—how had he left his own heart out of his calculations? What arrogance had blinded him to his vulnerability?

He loved her. Fire seemed to burn where his heart had once been, a fierce black fire that consumed him. What other woman would have responded to the test in such a way? She had been reluctant at first, but in the end her true worth had shone forth. Underneath that self-absorbed exterior that he had so arrogantly despised was a woman of enormous heart, of powerful courage, with wit and humour in the teeth of adversity…and with all that, she had imagination, vision, ingenuity.

Now he had seen her true self, the human soul that

had been disguised by the trappings of a too-easy life, by the tarnish of self-absorption. The circumstance he had helped to create had rubbed the tarnish away, and the precious metal glowed with its true colour.

She was pure gold, and he felt now that the touchstone of his heart had always unconsciously known it. Like Salik in the story he had told her, he had seen the image, and had determined to find his true beloved and make her his own.

How could he have imagined himself immune to her?

He shook his head. He had told himself that Noor needed to have the veneer stripped away, but had ignored the fact of his own blindness. He too had needed a stripping away—he had needed to remove the cold reason by which he had judged her, and see her as his heart saw her. He had had to learn that he, too, had a heart. And that his heart was a better judge of truth than his intellect.

She belonged to him. That was a central truth, flowing like golden lava from an eruption in his heart. He looked back on his grandfather's command now as an impertinence. How had the old man dared to order Bari to love his own heart's breath, his own life, his eyes? He felt now that even his grandfather's wanting him to marry her was theft.

What a fool he had been, risking everything in the madness of this enterprise! Could she love him now, when he had imposed such unnecessary suffering on her? When he had ranted at her, blamed her, and told her the great lie—that he did not love her? Would she ever understand that he had not known his own heart till now, but still had been driven by its dictates?

Had she whispered her love last night, or had he dreamed it? He had cried his heart's truth, and heard her cry in the same moment, and joy had flooded him till he nearly wept.

But now he doubted. Had he only heard what he wished to hear, that simultaneous echo of his feelings?

He had to get them off the island. He had delayed too long already. He had proved her over and over again, her strength, her soul, her courage—but had he made her love him, or hate him?

He shook his head in weary resignation at his own stupidity. What woman would love a man who had reduced her to such circumstances? How had he imagined the great magic would occur here, where he offered her nothing but hunger and uncertainty and backbreaking work?

Perhaps it had been his heart ruling him, even then. Faced with her determination not to marry him, offered the chance to keep her to himself, away from the world—had it been that?

Such blind foolishness was over now. If only it were not too late.

He lifted the object in his hand and turned a switch to test the function. A soft red glow told him that the machine was alive. He paused there for a moment, trying to foresee the consequences of this tiny movement of his thumb, but the future was blank. He could not see it.

Still, it had to be done. Bari broke the wire and pressed the switch. There was no going back now. A helicopter would be scrambled within the hour. Depending on their position, rescue would probably arrive by midday.

That would give him time, he hoped. Time to state his case, to learn if what he had heard in the night had been her own voice.

"Wow, you're really walking!"

The sleepy voice came from behind him. He restrained the impulse to hide what he held, his heart sinking. "Walking?"

"You've come a long way down the beach, you know. How does your leg feel?"

"Oh—fine. Much better. Noor…"

Sleepy, sensually drugged, Noor stood blinking in the glow of sunrise, trying to wake up. Bari had something bright yellow in his hand. It had an aerial and its red eye was flashing with life. Weird. Could a working mobile phone have washed in on the tide?

"What's that?"

"Ah—"

"Let me see?"

She reached for the object, and with a kind of helpless resignation he let her take it from his hand.

She read the letters stamped in the yellow plastic without comprehending for a moment, and then gasped. At once she was wide awake, adrenaline rushing through her.

"My God, it's an EPIRB! Where did it come from?"

The jolt of excitement made her heart thump. Bari was still silent, and she looked up at him with a broad smile. "Is it transmitting? Do you think it came from the same ship that lost all that cargo? My God, what *luck!*"

EPIRB meant Emergency Position Indicating Radio Beacon, she knew. Wherever it had come from, if it was indeed working, rescue wasn't far off!

Noor whooped with excitement, relief and sheer happiness. "They'll track it! They'll come, won't they? How soon, do you think? I wonder what ship it's from! Isn't this amazing? Did it just arrive on the tide?"

Her relief was tinged with just the lightest brush of disappointment. She had been happy here in a way she had never experienced in the outside world—the happiness of self-sufficiency and self-worth. And she had a sudden premonition that such happiness might not survive a return to the world. That what she had learned and decided here might not be sustainable in the whirl and pressure of that other life.

Bari was gazing out over the water, curiously still.

"Noor," he said softly. "Noor, I—"

"That's funny," she noticed absently. "The tide's only just starting to come in. When did this thing land?"

She peered at the yellow case in the early light. There was quite often an identifying label on an EPIRB, she knew from her yachting friends.

Al Khalid. Aircraft call sign ISQ26. Aircraft registration...

"What on earth—!"

Noor's eyes widened, narrowed, and then squeezed tightly shut, her face twisting into denial as she understood.

"Is this—*yours?*" She opened her eyes again and gazed at him in disbelief.

"Yes," he said, and in one bright flash she saw it all. The whole picture.

"You *can't* have!" she breathed. "You *didn't!*" Her voice broke on anguish. "Oh, God!"

"Noor, I love you," he said, too late.

He tried to draw her into his arms, but like a wild animal she wrenched herself free of his hold and stepped back, staring at him, her face white.

"You had an EPIRB the whole time?" she whispered. "Right from the beginning, when we were in the raft? *Tell me!*" she shouted when he made no answer.

"You know it," Bari replied, taking it from her trembling palm and setting it on the sand to beam its message to the stars.

"We could have been rescued as soon as the storm was over. Before we even got to the island!"

She stared at him, her mind spinning with confusion and misery.

"What was it—an experiment? You were trying to see if you could break me? You wanted to—to... And now, for some reason—" she gestured to the EPIRB "—now the game's over and you're letting me go home! I wonder why?"

"I love you," Bari said urgently, for how could he believe that his love, which had changed everything for him, would have no power over her?

"No, that's not it!" she said in dismissive contempt. "That's not why you're calling a halt." She frowned, her mind whirling, trying to see her way through the jumble of impressions. "No, what changed between last night and this morning? Just one thing—I told you I loved you."

Noor closed her eyes, the ice-water truth of it coursing through her blood. "That's what you were waiting for, isn't it? That's what you planned here—a little *Taming of the Shrew.* Brainwash her, break her down, and *hey presto!* She'll think she loves you!"

"No!" he protested, but it sounded like a lie.

"Rescue was going to arrive by chance, wasn't it? You'd have found some explanation, and I'd never have known! Only, I woke up early."

"I hadn't even considered what to tell you," he said levelly. "Please lis—"

"*Bullshit* you hadn't! You'd considered the whole damned thing from beginning to end! You started plotting this—when? When we were still in the plane? Boy, nobody crosses you and gets away with it, do they? What was it—the breaking of Noor Ashkani's spirit as prelude to a loveless marriage?"

"You are not broken," he said, emphasizing each

word. "And I planned nothing. I took advantage of the situation. I admit it. But—"

"I suppose you even faked the wounded leg!" she accused.

He suddenly lost his grip on himself. "Try to keep your accusations within limits!" he advised angrily.

"You're walking now and you look pretty comfortable!"

"I've been able to walk for the past—"

"And I notice, belatedly I admit, that last night it didn't give you many problems!"

Last night. Her breath hissed in through her teeth. "You really wanted to make me your slave in every way, didn't you?" she whispered. "Did you enjoy having me fetch and carry for you? Are you happy? Was revenge tasty? And now we'll go back to civilization—though nowhere can be called civilization, exactly, if you're there—and then what?"

He abandoned his anger and said urgently, "Noor, don't take it like this. Think of what you learned during this time. Think of what you know!"

"Learned? I learned what kind of…of self-satisfied, arrogant *bastard* you are!"

His jaw clenched. "That is not all you learned."

"Screw you."

She turned away, taking in the sight of their campsite, the little shelter, the fireplace, the stacks of salvage…the place that, she realized suddenly, had come to mean home to her, because Bari was there. The place where she had learned to rise to the challenge, where she had responded to necessity with invention, where she had learned what she could do, where she had discovered…

Now she suddenly saw it as an outsider would see it: a primitive place—a filthy, half-blackened, jerry-built shack, a stack of ragged boxes, an overturned half-deflated life raft, the detritus of the fire, the bubble wrap that served as their mattress…. And most primitive of all—herself, a half-naked savage with ratty hair, peeling face, scratched, scabbed arms and legs, sunburned skin, wearing a dirty scrap of once-white silk…

And a pathetic, handmade string of pearls around her neck.

That, suddenly, was the worst humiliation of all.

Noor's stomach heaved. She had been so pleased with it, with herself for making it, had modelled it for Bari with such pride!

With choking revulsion, she lifted her hands and tore at the necklace. The fishing line was too strong to break, but at her ferocious jerking the knot slipped and gave at last. The pearls spilled into the sand at his feet, one by one.

Noor turned on her heel and headed toward the hut.

"Listen to me!" His hand caught her wrist, and he forced her to face him again.

Her jaw was clamped tight against tears, but her eyes were shuttered, showing no way in.

He had to try. "Did I have no excuse for what I have done, Noor? I don't say I was right. It was an insane thing—but remember what had happened. Remember your own actions when you remember mine. I offered you marriage in good faith, believing that, if we didn't love each other, still we could make a strong partnership. I had made up my mind that you were my life's partner, the mother of my children. The whole of my world was there to witness that. And then the guard came to tell me you had been seen driving away in the limousine…. Did I have no excuse for anger? For madness, even?"

It made no impact, he could see that. Noor stood

straight and cold. "You've had plenty of time to get over it, too. Are you trying to tell me you only now came to your senses?"

"Perhaps. They call love a madness—they say a lover is a madman. But for me perhaps it is the other way. Maybe learning that I love you brought me to my senses at last. Because I have learned it."

She snorted. "Oh, do me a favour!"

"Noor, let us stop this before it leads to a path that neither of us can turn back from! We have each done terrible things to the other. Let us forget those hurts, in the name of love. I love you. You are my woman, my wife."

"Oh, this from the guy who wouldn't even lend me his jacket till I got on my knees and begged!" she recalled with renewed bitterness. "What it means to be the woman of Bari al Khalid, eh?"

"You love me," he said. "You said it, last night."

She laughed mirthlessly. "Don't you believe it! Aren't you the man who said women always talk like that during sex?"

"Not you, however."

"Ah, but I've been trained by a master! And I'm a quick study, as you've noticed yourself. But don't forget you also once called me heartless. If you brought me here in the hopes of breaking me down to the point of being willing to marry you," Noor said, opening her eyes at him, "sorry, but you were a little premature with the EPIRB. Maybe you shou—"

She broke off when he wrapped his arms around her and dragged her tight against his body. Fierce black eyes burned her for a moment, and then his mouth smothered hers.

Her blood went up like gunpowder, but before the heat could reach her brain, Noor tore her mouth away.

"Don't touch me!"

"Show me how you have been hurt by what I did, and I will let you go!" he declared fiercely, delivering kisses behind her ear, on her throat, in her hair as she twisted her face away. "Noor, I love you!"

Even in the heat of her anguish, his mouth could ignite her blood. Her heart beat in a wild, thrilling tattoo, as if it believed his love. Her body felt the strength of his hold, the hunger of his hands, read the passion in his eyes, and leaped from desire to hunger to drowning passion in a moment. She was melting for him as if she had made no terrible discovery between last night's lovemaking and this moment.

"Marry me, Noor!" he begged, his voice growling in his throat. "I love you, I want you. You are mine!"

From some distant coldness in her, she found the strength to thrust him from her. "Don't touch me again," she ordered coldly. "Don't even speak to me."

Fifteen

"**O**w! Ah, ooh! Oh, don't stop, Rudayba, it's wonderful! *Yow,* that hurt! Oh, did I ever—*aaah!*—miss this!"

The full-body Shiatsu Massage with Cucumber and Nine Essential Oils was just what Noor needed, and if it brought tears to her eyes, who would look further for the cause?

Her cousin Jalia, that was who.

"So what now—you're not speaking to him?" Jalia was sitting on the sofa by Noor's head, lazily flicking through a pile of newspapers and magazines. The two cousins were in her suite in the palace, hiding out from Bari and, incidentally, from the media. Noor's adventure was the kind of fodder the tabloids and celebrity magazines fed on, and they had smelled blood.

"Do you *expect* me to speak to him?"

Jalia shrugged. "I don't get you. You were willing to marry him when you didn't love him and he'd never said he loved you. Now he insists he's crazy about you, and you're breaking your heart for love of him—"

"I am not!"

"—but now you won't hear of marriage. There's a certain lack of fundamental logic, isn't there?"

"I told you, Jalia," Noor repeated doggedly. "When I said I'd marry him, I was so hypnotized I didn't even realize that what I felt wasn't love. On the island I thought I'd learned to love him, but that was just brainwashing, wasn't it? It's not real love."

"Keep saying that, and you might even come to believe it. There's more than one way to get indoctrinated. You can even do it to yourself."

"That is just so ridiculous!"

"You're a very different person from the Noor I used to know. I told you before. Your eyes smile. You're…considerate. Is that why you're so mad at Bari?"

Noor took a deep breath against the pain Rudayba was inflicting. "No," she said softly. "No, I'm…I'm aware of that, and I'm grateful for it. But that doesn't mean—" She blew out a hopeless breath.

Jalia shrugged and lifted up the magazine she was flicking through to show Noor the double-page spread. RETURN OF THE CASTAWAY PRINCESS!

There were several photos of Noor and Bari climbing out of the rescue helicopter, their faces strained and worn, enveloped in the robes their rescuers had given them. In one of them the little rag doll was visible on Noor's arm—the only thing Noor had carried with her from the island.

A few library photos filled up the rest of the space, the magazine's attempt to disguise the fact that there was nothing apart from the fact of the rescue to write about. Neither Noor nor Bari had given any interviews yet, in spite of pestering that amounted to persecution. And considering her own family's response to her story, Noor wasn't at all eager to make explanations to the broader public. Her mother hadn't spoken to her for an entire day.

"They want the next instalment, and they won't wait forever. What are you going to tell everybody? The truth?"

"Ow! Ow! Rudayba, that one's really—*Ya Allah!* Ooh, that's good! No, are you kidding?" Noor continued to Jalia in English without a break. "The truth? *He Never Loved Me, Sobs Broken-Hearted Princess?* I *don't* think!"

"Of course, you could always sue him." Jalia tossed the magazine aside and picked up a newspaper. WEDDING FLIGHT MYSTERY STILL UNEXPLAINED, Noor read. "They'd love you if you did."

"Sue him for what?" Noor demanded irritably.

"Involuntary forced confinement, of course. The media would gorge on that. You could give them all the details of the hardship your villainous, mercenary fiancé put you through, trying to break your indomitable spirit."

"Rudayba, that's enough digging for one day, thanks," Noor said suddenly. The masseuse stopped, wiped her hands and discreetly left. Noor clambered off the table, wrapping the gigantic white towel around her. Cleanliness still seemed an unparalleled luxury.

"I'm going to take a shower."

Jalia obediently followed her into the bathroom, where Noor examined herself in the mirror. After several days of serious facial and skin rejuvenation work, she was looking human again. Her hair squeaked, her hands had been soaked and scrubbed till her fingertips were nearly raw, the nails were neatly rounded and glossily polished. Her feet were similarly restored.

Various bruises and scratches were fading along with the aches and pains. In fact, it was back to her old life again.

The only things that didn't fade were the memories. When she closed her eyes she still saw Bari's face, felt his hands, his mouth…when she breathed her heart still ached.

"So, you want to call a lawyer?" Jalia flung herself into a plush chair as Noor started the shower.

"Don't be ridiculous. I'm not going to sue Bari!"

"Why not?"

Noor smiled sweetly. "Because that would require seeing him in court."

"That bad, huh?"

Noor stepped under the water and picked up the plastic bottle of perfumed shower scrub. She stood looking at it for a moment before shooting the soft green liquid into her palm. How she had yearned to be here then, but somehow now…she would give anything to be back on the island, falling in love with Bari and believing that he was falling in love with her.

She felt tears burn her eyes and quickly pushed her face under the stream, rubbing the lather into her breasts, her neck, her arms, her stomach, fiercely trying to blank out the memory of that day by the falls.

But a brand isn't got rid of so easily.

"If you don't agree to see me, I'll give an interview to the media," Bari's voice threatened. Noor tried to pretend to herself that she could listen to his voice without melting.

"And why should I care?"

"You might not like what I'm going to tell them. I plan to say you ran away because you were only marrying me for my money, and at the last minute you learned the family property was less than you thought."

"What? Who'd believe that?"

"The media don't care about the truth, they care about a story. I can make the story look good. On the other hand, if we were to talk, we might come up with an even better story to give them."

"Are you threatening me? Is this blackmail?"

"You aren't surprised, are you? You already know I'll stop at nothing."

"Why are you doing this?" Noor shouted. "What do you *want?*"

"That's easy. I thought you knew. I want you. Now, and forever."

Her heart thundered. "Well, you can't have me," Noor said doggedly. Then, because she couldn't resist, "And anyway, how would telling a bunch of media types that I was marrying you for your money help you?"

"Isn't it obvious? The only way you'll be able to redeem yourself in the world's eyes after a statement like that is by marrying me."

She slammed the phone down.

"Princess, how do you feel about Jabir al Khalid's ultimatum?"

The journalist had cracked her cell phone code and Noor had been fooled into answering. Now she was trapped.

She hesitated, wondering how to get the maximum information from the journalist while giving the minimum away. She was not experienced in dealing with the media, and she knew she should get off the phone as quickly as possible without offending the woman.

But she was wild to know what Bari's opening salvo was.

So she laughed lightly. "I don't really know what you're referring to. Ultimatum?" Had Bari told the media about his grandfather?

"I'm talking about his discovery that you aren't, after all, the granddaughter of his old friend."

Noor's jaw fell open. "That I'm...what?"

"Didn't you know, Princess? It seems the old man thought you were the descendant of his best friend, and that's why he approved of the marriage between you and Bari. But now he's discovered that he had confused the names. Not so surprising at his age, I imagine. It turns out your grandfather, Faruq Durrani, was the Sheikh's fellow Cup Companion, all right, but not his special friend."

"Really?" Noor prompted, curious to know where this was leading.

"In fact, as I understand it, your grandfather was actually Jabir al Khalid's rival in love. And Faruq Durrani won. Somehow Jabir al Khalid got the name of his enemy confused with the name of his friend."

She paused compellingly.

"I guess memory can do funny things." Noor knew enough to fill the gap with a platitude. She was unsure whether to believe this, but what was the point?

"Now that he's remembered, apparently, he doesn't want his grandson to marry you?" the reporter said, on a rising note.

"What?"

"Jabir al Khalid has changed his mind about wanting Bari to marry you, apparently."

Noor sat stunned, the phone pressed to her ear. Was it true? Bari forbidden to marry her? Her heart nearly stopped at the thought. She lifted her mouth away from the receiver and tried to breathe quietly, sucking in gulps of air, fighting for calm.

"Uh, it's a surprise to me," she said when she could.

"It's not true? Are you and Bari still engaged?"

"I think that's for Bari and me to decide."

"Because I hear the man who really was Bari's grandfather's friend has five granddaughters, and Bari is supposed to choose from them."

"No comment," Noor whispered.

"Why didn't you and Bari get married, Princess?"

Noor put the phone down.

She paced the suite, racked with indecision and torment.

Could it be true? Had the old man made such a discovery? Or was this just the first salvo in the war Bari had promised her?

But when her mother called to tell her the same story, she had to believe it: Bari's grandfather had made a mistake. He now saw the halting of the wedding—whatever had caused it—as a gift from God. And he intended to accept the gift. Bari was forbidden to marry Noor, who was the granddaughter of a villain.

Noor's mother had been furious enough before. Now her air of reproach was almost more than Noor could stand.

"Do you think—will he do it?" Noor asked, trying for calm.

"Of course he will obey his grandfather, as is fitting. He did so before—why should he resist now? If he wants the property, he must!" her mother said bitterly. "You have thrown away such a man, Noor, and your choice is sadly very final. If the marriage had been completed, the old man would probably never have remembered his error, or if he did, it would have been when he had a great-grandchild on his knee, and too much happiness to regret it. Now—"

It was the first time her mother had ever spoken to her in such a tone. The first time, she supposed, that she had ever seriously disappointed her mother's very low expectations of her. What had been asked of Noor? That she enjoy herself and marry well. And she had screwed up.

What a fool she was. She understood herself now, when it might be too late. Because the thought that Bari might marry *her* simply in order to inherit the family estates was nothing compared to the horror of thinking he might marry some other woman for the same reason.

Sixteen

Noor dressed carefully for his visit, in a neat navy linen suit with a pencil skirt that emphasized her slimmed-down figure, a white tank top under the smart jacket, bare legs and sling-back stilettos.

She was sitting at a table by the window, examining an engineering college course catalogue, when Bari was admitted by her maid. She pretended not to notice his entrance, turning a page noisily.

A dark hand entered her field of vision and closed on the page. A second later the book was ripped from her slackened grasp and sent flying across the room.

Noor's eyes swept up and hungrily took in the sight of him for the first time since they had left the island. The beard was gone, the dark hair neatly cut and curling. He was wearing casual Western dress—tan jeans, loafers and a black polo shirt that revealed his dark, muscled arms, his smooth throat.

She opened her mouth to complain, but Bari beat her to it.

"I don't have time for your games," he warned. "You called me here. What do you want?"

He gripped her arms and drew her to her feet. In her high heels, her eyes on a level with his, she gazed into the black depths with expectant alarm.

Muttering an oath, he swept her into his embrace, and his mouth clamped itself to hers, firm and silky, hungry and hot. His arms imprisoned her, velvet-covered steel: at the same time hard, so that she couldn't escape, and soft, so that she didn't want to.

Her blood boiled up under his touch; her mouth felt swollen with pleasure and yearning. His tongue teased its way past her tingling lips with tender electricity that ran everywhere through her body. His arm clamped her waist, his other hand cupped her head, the fingers threading through her hair.

It wasn't, it just wasn't possible to resist him, Noor admitted helplessly. This might be their last kiss. Was it their last kiss? Was he going to marry someone else?

His kiss grew fiercer, more possessive, his arm sliding behind her head and locking her in the curve of his elbow, the other hand gripping her waist, then her hip, then wrapping right around her back under the jacket to clasp her tightly against him. Noor found herself tilted crazily backwards over his arm as he kissed her ruthlessly. She was half fainting from pleasure and the fact that the world was upside down.

Her arms encircled his neck in luxurious hunger, her breasts pressed against him. She moaned as his mouth left hers and trailed down her neck to the perfumed pulse in the base of her throat.

"At least I smell better than the last time you kissed me," she said stupidly.

"Do you think I like perfume better than the scent of your body?" he growled, and his mouth moved up to smother hers again.

It was some time before she could ask him the questions she had summoned him to ask, and when she got around to it, she was on his lap, while he sat on the sofa. Her shoes were off, her skirt hiked up, his hand caressing her inner thigh, just above the knee, with a touch that melted her.

"It's no setup," Bari said, shaking his head at her accusation. "Grandfather made a mistake. It was while the media were asking questions about us when we were missing, and he began to talk about his old friend, that he suddenly got the names straight in his mind. And he remembered that your grandfather wasn't his dear friend after all, but the one who had stolen his lady love, one of the al Jawadi princesses, and married her."

"How could he make such a mistake? Didn't he have the details checked out?" Noor protested.

"He got the two names confused in his memory, that's all. It was a long time ago, and he's an old man. I have an idea that subconsciously he wanted me to marry the granddaughter of the woman he once loved. But now that he's realized the truth, he won't be acting on an unconscious motive any longer. And he's as determined as ever to run my life."

She held her breath.

Bari drew her hand to his lips and kissed the knuckles, then the palm. "He forbids our marriage, Noor. In marrying you, I'll lose my birthright. I'll have little to offer you materially. What my father left me doesn't compare with what is in my grandfather's control. But the task is still the same—to rebuild the country, with the tools that come to our hands." He looked up into her face, his love written in his eyes. "Will you do that with me? Will you marry me?"

Noor bit her lip. "Why don't you just—marry that other man's granddaughter, the way your grandfather wants?"

"Because I love you," he told her, giving her a little shake. "Because you are a woman without equal, and I want to be the father of your children. Because life is empty without you, Noor, and the palaces and lands and wealth I would inherit if I obeyed my grandfather could not fill the emptiness."

Her heart kicked so hard her breast ached. How she wanted to believe him. But…

"Oh, Bari!" she whispered, her eyes troubled.

He breathed deep, as if she had struck him a blow over the heart. "I understand," he said. "Will you listen while I try to explain, Noor? It isn't much of an explanation, but…I'm asking for your understanding—and forgiveness."

She gazed at him wordlessly. His hand gently stroked her hip.

"I was very angry with you, Noor. It's no good trying to gloss it over. So angry that even when I was hiding at the back of the plane, and heard that the airport was socked in, a part of me was hoping the shock would teach you a lesson. Even at that point I was tempted to leave you in the dilemma for a while. So you see the idea was already in the back of my mind, that you should be allowed to lie in the bed you had made."

He paused, gathering his thoughts. "I had forgotten that there was an EPIRB in the plane's grab bag. I suppose I didn't think of it because there wasn't much urgency about it. No one could have scrambled a helicopter during the storm even if we had been transmitting. Whereas what we were doing was immediately essential to our survival."

"But when the storm was over, I asked you about an EPIRB. I remember."

"And I remembered then, and lied about it. Almost instinctively. I thought—this situation is a learning opportunity, but the lesson hasn't hit home with her at all."

She nodded ruefully. "I was just expecting that life would get right back to normal and I wouldn't have to adjust, so what was the point?"

He drew her hand to his mouth and kissed it thoughtfully. "I didn't get the whole picture at once. I just decided to see how you would react to a little more hardship. It wasn't until that night that…"

He paused.

"That night?"

"I want to tell you a part of my life that I haven't told you before," Bari offered softly, and when she nodded intently, he began.

"My father died when I was fifteen. It had been the dream of his life to return to live in Bagestan one day. When he was dying, he asked me to promise that I would help to further the royal family's attempts to regain their throne, and one day, when it became possible, return and restore the family property and make my home here. He knew his father would leave me what would have been his own inheritance. I swore to him that I would do as he wished. I meant it. I became committed in that moment."

Noor thought of her own parents' passion for their troubled country, a passion that had survived time and distance, and that, without her consciously realizing it, they had passed on to her.

"I know," she said softly.

"It was always understood between my grandfather and me that, while I would certainly not inherit all the family property, I would undertake to reclaim and restore it on behalf of us all. And I would have the money to do it.

"After the Return, my grandfather suddenly made conditions. I proposed to you, Noor, believing that I had no choice. I owed it to my own hopes, to my father and the promise I had made him.

"But that night on the island, I began to consider whether I was prepared to sacrifice my hope of a happy marriage for the sake of that promise. Whether my father would have wanted me to make such a sacrifice. If I was going to make you change your mind again—"

"Oh, just like that?" Noor said dangerously.

He smiled unrepentantly and touched her cheek. "You'd changed it once already, remember. It was at least possible. But—should I make the attempt? That was the question. When I proposed to you, I had believed that in spite of everything you were someone with whom I could make a good marriage. When you ran from the wedding…"

Noor bit her lip. "You should hear my mother on the subject!"

"…I asked myself if that judgement had been mistaken, if we were too different in outlook to make the kind of partnership I envisaged happen. And it was while I was turning that over in my mind that I realized that—" he paused "—that I had been given an opportunity to find out who you truly were."

"Not to make me love you?"

"That, too, if I could." He stretched up and kissed her. "What I didn't realize was how much of an opportunity it would be for me to learn about myself. And my own heart."

They were quiet for a moment. "And so you…you just decided to keep me there till…what?"

"I didn't think that far ahead. I just went from day to day, and after a while I almost forgot about the EPIRB. It didn't seem relevant. Until the day we got the flotsam. I was out there in the water with my leg cut open, fighting to hold that rope, determined to get those crates, and I suddenly thought—what the hell am I doing? There could be sharks out here, and I'm risking that for a few crates of food when we can call for rescue any time?"

A laugh escaped her. "Why didn't you get the EPIRB then? You were badly hurt. Weren't you scared?"

He kissed her again. "Can't you guess? Because I couldn't walk to the hiding place! I'd have had to tell you about it, and I knew how you would react. How hurt you would be. I thought—I can never explain it. But even then I didn't understand that I couldn't hurt you because I loved you."

His hands tightened on her, but Noor resisted. "But later, when you were walking again? It must have been uncomfortable. Why not then? Where was it hidden?"

"It wasn't far. But by then, Noor, you were in the middle of a metamorphosis. You were suddenly finding what you could really do. And I couldn't interrupt your journey.

"Now tell me your side of it," he said.

Noor heaved a sigh. "I learned so much, Bari. You're right, it was a kind of metamorphosis. I hated a lot of it, but—I guess that was the price of change. And I can't be sorry it happened."

"Do you forgive me, Noor?"

She smiled into his eyes. "How can I be grateful for

what happened and still blame the person who caused it? Yes, I forgive you. Can you forgive me?"

For answer, he wrapped her head with strong, possessive hands and lay back, drawing her down to his hungry kiss. When she lifted herself away from him again, he held her face and whispered, looking into her eyes, "And…do you love me? Will you marry me, Beloved?"

She closed her eyes against the thundering of her own heart, then opened them again.

"No answer?" he begged hoarsely.

"I love you, Bari." The words seemed torn from her throat. "Yes, yes, how could I say no?"

The strength roared into him, and he kissed her with a rough and hungry passion that ignited her blood, burned her, melted her. They slipped down into the soft sofa, arms and legs entwining, wild hunger in their hearts and mouths.

After a moment, he drew his head away. "First things first," he whispered, reaching into his pocket. When he lifted his hand, he was holding the beautiful diamond solitaire that had been her engagement ring.

Noor suddenly remembered the piercing, painful moment on her wedding day when she had torn it off her finger—a different woman, in another lifetime.

"Give me your hand," Bari commanded in a gravel voice. Noor breathed deep, lifted her left hand and put it in his.

With a look of passionate possessiveness, the Sheikh slipped his ring back where it belonged.

A long time later, he murmured, "Do you remember the day I took you sailing down the coast?"

She was on the bed in the curve of Bari's arm, leaning over him on one elbow as he lay back against the pillows, sweat-damp curls falling on his forehead, his eyes lazy with love.

She gave him a look. Remember?

"The house up above—do you remember it? It is a beautiful place, or it was once."

"Oh!" Noor whispered. "And it's—your family's?"

"That particular property was left to me by my father. I meant to show it to you that day. But—we did other things."

"Did we? I've forgotten," Noor teased, and then fell down onto his warm chest and was thoroughly kissed for her pains.

"It will fall into the sea if repairs are not undertaken soon," he said then. "Although of course we must have somewhere in the city, I would like to restore that as our home. Will you come with me now and look at it, and see if you would like to live there?"

"Yes, but what are we going to tell the media? They're all out there, and when they see us together…" Noor gabbled anxiously.

"We can't let them publish the truth," he said.

She nodded in vigorous relief. "It would make me look like such an idiot. I mean, I *was* a fool, but do I have to be exposed as one in front of the world?"

Bari leaned up and kissed her. "Don't call my beloved names."

"Not in public, anyway," Noor agreed with a grin. "Is there some explanation we could make that would satisfy the media and put them off the scent?"

Bari's eyes glinted thoughtfully. "My grandfather's foolishness has had many uses," he mused. "With his first decree, he found you for me, and with his second, he brought you back to me. And I really don't think he will have the right to complain if we make use of him again!"

Epilogue

"THE PRINCESS I LOVE!"
Forbidden Wedding Will Go Ahead!

The marriage of Cup Companion Sheikh Bari al Khalid and Princess Noor Yasmin al Jawadi Durrani, which was dramatically halted in Bagestan last month when the bride and groom mysteriously disappeared, is on again, according to sources.

The truth behind the mystery of the wedding couple's disappearance, only minutes before the ceremony was due to begin, has at last come out. Sources close to the couple have revealed that the Princess and her fiancé fled because Sheikh Jabir al Khalid, the groom's grandfather, dramatically withdrew his permission and barred the union at the eleventh hour. The couple fled, intending to undertake the ceremony elsewhere. But their plane was forced down in a storm, and the rest is history. The couple spent what would have been their honeymoon on an uninhabited island, surviving on turtle eggs.

Their disappearance, the search, the dramatic rescue, and the couple's continuing devotion have had no influence on the old Sheikh's decision, however.

Bari al Khalid will be forced to sacrifice his expected inheritance, consisting of vast property in Bagestan, in order to marry the woman he loves. The legacy will now probably go to a cousin.

"My wife and I will build a new legacy together," the handsome Cup Companion has been quoted as saying. The wedding is expected to take place next month.

* * * * *

Look for Princess Jalia's story,
THE ICE MAIDEN'S SHEIKH,
the next book in the **SONS OF THE DESERT** *series,*
from Alexandra Sellers,
in December 2004.

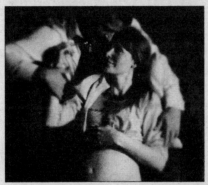

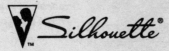

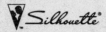

INTIMATE MOMENTS™

and

Linda Winstead Jones

present

**When your back's against the wall
and your heart's on the line...**

Running Scared

(Intimate Moments #1334)

In the jungles of South America, Quinn Calhoun
must rescue impetuous Olivia Larkin from the
dangerous hurricane of corruption, kidnappings and
murder that whirls around her. But protecting her
means spending time in *very* close quarters....

Available December 2004 at your favorite retail outlet.

And look for the next LAST CHANCE HEROES title,
Truly, Madly, Dangerously (IM #1348), in February 2005.

COMING NEXT MONTH

#1621 SHOCKING THE SENATOR—Leanne Banks
Dynasties: The Danforths
Abraham Danforth had tried to deny his attraction to his campaign manager, Nicola Granville, for months—although they *had* shared a secret night of passion. With the election won and Abraham becoming Georgia's new senator, would the child Nicola now carried become the scandal that would ruin his career?

#1622 WILD IN THE MOMENT—Jennifer Greene
The Scent of Lavender
The whirring blizzard, the cracking fire and their intimate quarters had Daisy Campbell and Teague Larson unexpectedly sharing a wild moment. The two hardly seemed like a match made in heaven...so why couldn't Daisy turn down Teague's surprise business deal and *many more* wild moments?

#1623 THE ICE MAIDEN'S SHEIKH—Alexandra Sellers
Sons of the Desert
Beauty Jalia Shahbazi had been a princess-under-wraps for twenty-seven years and that was how she planned to keep it. That was until sexy Sheikh Latif Al Razzaqi Shahin awakened her Middle Eastern roots... and her passion. But Latif wanted to lay claim to more than Jalia's body— and she dared not offer more.

#1624 FORBIDDEN PASSION—Emilie Rose
Lynn Riggan's brother-in-law Sawyer was everything her recently deceased husband was not: caring, giving and loving. The last thing Lynn was looking for was forbidden passion, but after briefly giving in to their intense mutual attraction, she couldn't get Sawyer out of her head... or her heart. Might an unexpected arrival give her all she'd ever wanted?

#1625 RIDING THE STORM—Brenda Jackson
Jayla Coles had met many Mr. Wrongs when she finally settled on visiting the sperm bank to get what she wanted. Then she met the perfect storm— fire captain Storm Westmoreland. They planned on a no-strings-attached affair, but their brief encounter left them with more than just lasting memories....

#1626 THE SEDUCTION REQUEST—Michelle Celmer
Millionaire restaurateur Matt Conway returned to his hometown to prove he'd attained ultimate success. But when he ran into former best friend and lover, Emily Douglas, winning over her affection became his number-one priority. Problem was, she was planning on marrying another man...and Matt was just the guy to make her change her mind.

SDCNM1104